Ryan moved a step toward her

Annie sat very still.

"I meant what I said on the river today. I want to give what's between us a shot."

"There's nothing between us," she denied, jumping to her feet, intending to return to the house. Instead of backing away, he took a step forward, trapping her between the picnic table and his body.

"You know that's not true." He laid a hand against her cheek. "You can feel it, the same way I do. There's always been something there."

Dear Reader,

As a reader, nothing pulls me into a story more effectively than a secret. That's probably why my own books tend to be full of them. It's great fun to uncover the mystery along with the characters. It's almost as enjoyable when one character keeps something from another.

In most books with a plot involving a secret baby, the father is the one who's in the dark. In *The Secret Sin,* it's the baby herself, who's grown into a lovely thirteen-year-old girl.

Lindsey Thompson has no idea she's on a collision course with her birth parents when she runs away to Indigo Springs to visit a family friend—or the effect she'll have on the two former lovers who haven't spoken in fourteen years.

I hope you enjoy the third book in the RETURN TO INDIGO SPRINGS series, with the couple who will do anything to keep their birth daughter from getting hurt.

All my best,

Darlene Gardner

THE SECRET SIN
Darlene Gardner

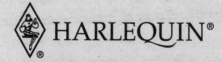

HARLEQUIN®

TORONTO • NEW YORK • LONDON
AMSTERDAM • PARIS • SYDNEY • HAMBURG
STOCKHOLM • ATHENS • TOKYO • MILAN • MADRID
PRAGUE • WARSAW • BUDAPEST • AUCKLAND

Recycling programs
for this product may
not exist in your area.

ISBN-13: 978-0-373-78325-0

THE SECRET SIN

Copyright © 2009 by Darlene Hrobak Gardner.

ABOUT THE AUTHOR

While working as a newspaper sportswriter, Darlene Gardner realized she'd rather make up quotes than rely on an athlete to say something interesting. So she quit her job and concentrated on a fiction career that landed her at Harlequin/Silhouette Books, where she wrote for Harlequin Temptation, Harlequin Duets and Silhouette Intimate Moments before finding a home at Harlequin Superromance. Please visit Darlene on the Web at www.darlenegardner.com.

Books by Darlene Gardner

HARLEQUIN SUPERROMANCE

1316–MILLION TO ONE
1360–A TIME TO FORGIVE
1396–A TIME TO COME HOME
1431–THE OTHER WOMAN'S SON
1490–ANYTHING FOR HER CHILDREN
1544–THE HERO'S SIN*
1562–THE STRANGER'S SIN*

*Return to Indigo Springs

Don't miss any of our special offers. Write to us at the following address for information on our newest releases.

Harlequin Reader Service
U.S.: 3010 Walden Ave., P.O. Box 1325, Buffalo, NY 14269
Canadian: P.O. Box 609, Fort Erie, Ont. L2A 5X3

To Kurt, Paige and Brian—the loves of my life.

CHAPTER ONE

ANNIE SUBLINSKI gulped down the last bite of her turkey sandwich and scooped her sunglasses off the kitchen counter before grabbing the receiver on the ringing telephone.

This was the third time she'd had to answer the phone in the last ten minutes, proving that her father was right. He did need her to take time away from her magazine-writing career to be in charge of Indigo River Rafters while he was away.

She didn't bother with a hello. "What is it this time, Jason?"

She'd instructed the teenager her father had hired for the summer to prepare the next group of white-water rafters for the one o'clock run down the Lehigh. He was a nice enough kid, but she wouldn't be surprised if he couldn't locate the paddles. So far he'd phoned asking first where to find the liability forms and then the sunscreen they sold in the shop.

The silence that carried over the line was uncharacteristic for Jason, whose weak point wasn't lack of communication.

"I was calling my uncle Frank." The voice, young and female, was not one Annie could identify.

Annie's father's first name was Frank. If the girl had spoken with a Polish accent and called her father *Wujeck Franek,* she'd conclude it was one of his nieces. But wouldn't they know he was visiting their family in Kraków?

"I must have the wrong number," the girl continued, providing an explanation; the call was a mistake.

"No problem." Annie hung up and headed for the door, instantly putting the girl out of her mind.

From the porch of her father's modest home, the warehouse-type building serving as company headquarters was visible, with the wide blue ribbon of river beyond it. The rafting trip she was leading wasn't scheduled to leave for another fifteen minutes, but she needed to brief her customers on the dos and don'ts of spending the afternoon on the rumbling river.

The phone sounded again, the shrill noise

stopping her in her tracks. It was probably the girl trying the number a second time. She debated ignoring it.

It continued to ring.

On the other hand, it could be Jason with a real crisis.

Just in case the few minutes it would take her to reach the shop mattered, she reversed course and plucked the receiver off the wall mount. "Yeah?"

"Oh. You again." It was the same young voice. "I thought I got the number right this time."

Annie twirled the stem of her polarized sunglasses in her free hand. She didn't have time for this. If she hadn't returned to her father's house to empty the dehumidifier and decided to wolf down lunch, she wouldn't even be here.

"What number are you calling?" she asked impatiently, then listened to the girl rattle off familiar digits.

"I'm positive that's the number Uncle Frank gave me," the girl said. "Are you sure this isn't the Sublinski residence?"

Annie stopped spinning her sunglasses. "This is the Sublinskis," she said slowly. "Who is this?"

"Lindsey Thompson."

The name meant nothing to Annie. Her mind reeled with possibilities of who the girl might be, none of which made sense. "How do you know my father?"

"Uncle Frank's your father?" It was the girl's turn to sound surprised. "He never said anything about having a daughter."

"He never told me about you, either," Annie said. "But you can't be his niece. All my father's nieces live in Poland."

"I'm not his real niece. I just call him Uncle Frank. He's friends with my grandpa Joe."

"Joe Thompson?"

"Joe Nowak."

The tension left Annie's coiled muscles. Her father often talked about his friend Joe. They'd known each other as boys in his native Poland. She seemed to recall that Joe lived in western Pennsylvania and had an adult daughter who'd died of breast cancer years ago. Her name had been…Helene. She searched her memory, certain her father had never mentioned Helene having children, but who else could this girl be? "Are you Helene's daughter?"

"Yes," the girl said. "So can I talk to Uncle Frank?"

"He's out of town," Annie said.

"You're kidding me?" She sounded distressed. "Now what am I going to do? He said I could come visit him anytime."

Visit him?

In the ensuing silence, Annie heard distant voices and what sounded like a train whistle. She got an uneasy feeling that Lindsey Thompson wasn't phoning from home.

"Where are you?" Annie asked.

"In Paoli." The town was on the westernmost edges of the Philadelphia suburbs, almost a ninety-minute drive from Indigo Springs. "At the train station."

"Alone?" Annie asked.

"Yes." The tone of her voice spiked the way a very young child's might. She no longer sounded as poised and self-assured as she had a few moments ago.

"How old are you?" Annie asked, her stomach clenching in preparation for the answer.

"Fifteen."

Damn. That was way too young to be alone at a train station in a strange city, even if Paoli wasn't exactly an urban metropolis. "Can you get on a train and go back home?"

"I don't know," Lindsey said. "Probably not. I'm kind of short on cash."

"You need to phone your parents."

"No! That's a terrible idea." She sounded on the verge of panic. "Oh, God. What am I going to do?"

Annie's mind whirled until she came to a sudden, inevitable decision. "Here's what you're going to do. Go inside the train station, find a bench, sit down and don't move."

"Why?"

Annie glanced at the kitchen wall clock, which showed it was ten minutes until her white-water trip was due to leave. Ten minutes in which she needed to find someone to take over for her. Because, really, what choice did she have?

Lindsey Thompson was only fifteen years old.

"I'm on my way."

THE WOODEN BENCHES inside the Paoli train station were empty except for a young woman reading a paperback novel and wearing a V-neck wrap top in a bright, eye-catching pink.

Annie did a complete three-sixty, turning slowly to visually cover every inch of a station that was doing brisk business for a Friday afternoon.

Commuters who'd taken the early train home from Philadelphia walked quickly through the corridor, getting a head start on their weekends. Customers sipped from cardboard cups in the coffee shop. Soon-to-be travelers stood at ticket windows or navigated the automated machines. Not a single person looked like a marooned fifteen-year-old.

So where was Lindsey Thompson?

Annie's heart thudded harder than mallets pounding a drum.

She'd phoned the train station after she'd hung up with Lindsey, and asked the employee who answered to keep an eye on the girl but there was no guarantee that he had.

Her gaze fell once more on the young woman engrossed in her book, part of her face obscured by long, silky honey-brown hair. Annie marched toward her.

"Excuse me." Annie spoke loudly enough to pull the woman out of her fictional world. "Have you seen a teenage girl?"

The woman lifted her head, brushing her hair back to gaze at Annie out of sky-blue eyes as lovely as the rest of her face. She had been blessed with nearly perfect bone structure: high cheekbones, a narrow, well-shaped nose, a delicate chin and a full mouth.

"Are you Annie Sublinski?" the young woman asked.

The voice matched the one on the phone. Annie looked closer and realized that beneath the makeup was a girl younger than she'd first thought.

Much younger.

"I'm Annie." She couldn't contain her surprise. "Are you Lindsey?"

"Yep." The girl smiled at her, revealing enviable white teeth. "Thanks for coming. I've been waiting here, just like you told me to."

She marked her place with a bookmark and closed the paperback with a soft thump. Annie recognized the name on the book cover. The author wrote romantic stories about good-hearted teenage vampires, wildly popular among young girls.

Even though Lindsey Thompson didn't look her age, a young girl was exactly what she was.

Lindsey stuffed the book in an expensive-looking oversize bag that matched her top before getting to her feet. She wore metallic pink ballerina flats with her skinny jeans, but still topped Annie by a few inches. She was also model-thin.

"What's that on your face?" Lindsey asked, touching her own unblemished cheek.

The purplish mark on Annie's left cheek was about the size of a silver dollar but irregularly shaped. Because of the stares of strangers, Annie never quite managed to forget its existence. Most people she was meeting for the first time didn't mention it, though. She fought against taking offense.

"A port-wine stain," Annie said. "I was born with it."

"Why do you still have it?" Lindsey's stare grew more intense. "Can't you get rid of it?"

Enough, Annie decided, was enough.

"Let's see about getting you on a return train," she said. "Don't worry about being short on cash. I'll pay for the ticket."

"But I don't want to go back to Pittsburgh." In a flash of her mascara-coated eyelashes, Lindsey went from a girl who seemed on the verge of womanhood to a whining teen. "I want to go to Indigo Springs."

That answered one of Annie's questions. Lindsey Thompson was from Pittsburgh. Annie steeled herself against the girl's pout.

"Sorry, but I'm not set up for visitors." Running her father's business was a full-time job. Besides, Annie didn't know anything about taking care of a kid. At nearly thirty, she'd never even babysat.

"I didn't come to visit *you*," Lindsey retorted, her lower lip still thrust forward. "I came to visit Uncle Frank. When he gets back, he'll let me stay. You'll see."

"My father's not coming back until next month. He's in Poland."

Lindsey's pretty mouth, with its pink-tinted lips, dropped open. Her expression crumbled. "He never said anything about visiting Poland."

Frank Sublinski, it seemed, had been closemouthed about a lot of things. Annie had left her father a voice mail on his cell phone during the drive to Paoli and was still waiting to hear why he'd never told her the late Helene Nowak Thompson had a daughter who called him Uncle Frank.

"Wait here while I check the train schedule." Annie didn't give Lindsey a chance to object. She headed for a ticket window, keeping guilt at bay by assuring herself the girl would be better off back home in Pittsburgh where she belonged.

She returned in minutes to find Lindsey once again sitting on the bench, but this time her book remained in her trendy bag. Her slender arms were crossed over her chest, her mouth a flat line.

"There isn't a train to Pittsburgh today," Annie said.

Lindsey's lovely face lit up, her lips curling into a smile. "Then I guess I have to come to Indigo Springs with you, don't I?"

Annie tried to look as though the prospect didn't disconcert her. "I need to call your parents first and tell them you're spending the night with me."

"They were already okay with me staying with Uncle Frank. They'll be okay with me staying with you."

Lindsey avoided Annie's eyes, which put Annie on alert. Her father hadn't known Lindsey was coming for a visit; Lindsey's parents probably weren't aware of the fact, either.

"I still need to call them," Annie said.

"It'd be pretty hard to call them without the phone number." Lindsey slung her bag over her shoulder and started moving toward the exit, pulling a piece of designer luggage on wheels behind her.

Now what? If one of her father's employees openly defied her, Annie could threaten to dock their wages or to fire them. Neither tactic would work on Lindsey Thompson.

She blew out a breath, as annoyed with

herself as she was with Lindsey. She easily caught up to the teenager, then moved slightly ahead of her to give the illusion that she was in control.

"We're calling your parents when we get to Indigo Springs," Annie told her once they were outside the station. "We'll tell them you're coming home tomorrow."

Lindsey acted as though she hadn't heard her, her silence more oppressive than the midafternoon heat of the August day. Taking short steps, probably because her jeans were so tight, she trudged along, the wheels of her suitcase wobbling over the cracks in the sidewalk that led to the parking lot.

She was having so much trouble toting the thing Annie itched to pick it up and be done with it.

"I can carry your bag for you," Annie offered.

"I'll manage." Lindsey continued to struggle stubbornly with the suitcase so it seemed to take forever until they reached Annie's pickup, an eight-year-old Dodge Ram. The vehicle had held up well considering the odometer showed more than one hundred thousand miles.

"*That's* your ride?" Lindsey hung back as

though afraid the vehicle would roar to life as if they were in a Stephen King novel.

"That's my ride," Annie said. "The suitcase goes in the truck bed."

She expected Lindsey to leave the task to her but the girl surprised her, retracting the handle and then picking up the suitcase. With the muscles in her thin arms straining, she managed to lift the piece of luggage up and over the side of the truck.

Annie got into the driver's seat, reaching across the cab to unlock the passenger door. After a prolonged pause, Lindsey stepped gingerly onto the flat step before settling into the seat.

"It's easier to get in and out when you're not wearing tight pants," Annie said.

"Skinny jeans are in." Lindsey gave her the once-over. "You must not follow fashion."

Annie glanced down at what for her was normal attire for a day on the river: a sleeveless tank top, waterproof sandals, quick-dry shorts and her Indigo River Rafters cap.

"I was getting ready to guide a group down the Lehigh River when you called," Annie said, then could have kicked herself. She sounded like she was offering up an excuse for her appearance. She touched the port-wine stain on her left cheek.

"What kind of group?" Lindsey asked.

"White-water rafting." Annie dropped her hand and put the truck in gear. She noticed that Lindsey was gripping the door handle. "You ever done any?"

Lindsey shuddered. "I'm not the out-doorsy type."

Great, Annie thought, wondering what they'd talk about during the drive to Indigo Springs. She needn't have worried. Lindsey leaned her head against the headrest and closed her eyes as though exhaustion had struck her.

Annie started to switch the radio channel to her favorite country-and-western station, then thought better of it, afraid to wake up Lindsey. She considered phoning Jason but rationalized he wouldn't be shy about calling her if he had an emergency. The long, boring drive seemed to take forever until she finally exited the interstate highway and got on the twisting back roads that cut through the mountains to Indigo Springs. The summer-thick leaves on the tall trees hugging both sides of the pavement let through just a sprinkling of the sun's rays, casting most of the road in shadows. Lindsey stirred, alerting Annie that the girl was awake.

"We'll be there in a few minutes," Annie said. "Base camp is a couple of miles from town, down by the river."

Lindsey groaned. Now what did that mean? Lindsey had already stated she wasn't "the outdoorsy type," but did she not appreciate nature's beauty?

"It's really quite a pretty setting," Annie said.

Lindsey groaned again. Annie might be inexperienced in dealing with teenagers, but she wouldn't stand for rudeness. She turned to Lindsey, intending to set her straight. The teenager's head lolled to the side. Her eyes were open but her skin was deathly pale.

Annie's irritation instantly vanished. "What's wrong?"

"I don't feel so good." The girl's voice was low and sluggish, and her eyelids fluttered as though she might pass out.

The pickup was approaching the fork in the road that led either downhill to Indigo River Rafters or uphill to town. Annie's adrenaline kicked in. She took the turn as fast as she dared and headed uphill.

A short time later, she drove into the picturesque heart of Indigo Springs, where century-old stone buildings shared space with restaurants, businesses and retail shops catering primarily to tourists. She pulled the pickup to the curb in front of a pediatrician's office that sported a sign with blue block lettering and set the parking brake.

"I don't need to see a doctor." Lindsey had been repeating the statement since she'd found out their destination. "I already feel better."

She looked only slightly improved, her coloring verging on frighteningly pale instead of ghostly white.

"Humor me." Annie got out of the truck and slammed the door. She opened the passenger door and helped Lindsey down from the high bench seat, careful the girl didn't wobble when she navigated the step. She let go of Lindsey's elbow once they were on level ground, but stayed alert just in case the girl actually fainted.

"A pediatrician!" Lindsey exclaimed when she saw where Annie was leading her. "Can't I at least go to a regular doctor?"

"Pediatricians see children up to age eighteen."

"Pediatricians are for babies." Lindsey pointed half a block up the street to a row house with a stone facade that housed another doctor's office. "Why can't we go there?"

If a serious illness struck Annie on the spot, she'd still avoid Whitmore Family Practice, even if it meant driving to the next town while feverish and delusional.

It hadn't always been that way. She'd been a patient of Dr. Whitmore's until he'd died a few years back, leaving his daughter to run the practice. Although Indigo Springs was no longer a sleepy, small town but a tourist destination, most locals knew by now that Sierra Whitmore had broken her leg in a car accident, then called the most logical person to help her out.

Her brother Ryan Whitmore.

"Dr. Whitmore's office closes early on Friday afternoons," Annie said, relatively sure that was still the case. "So no more arguing. Let's go see the pediatrician."

Looking too weak to offer up another protest, Lindsey walked with Annie into a cheerful office that featured bright-blue carpeting and wallpaper decorated with clowns and balloons.

Annie blew out a soft breath, silently congratulating herself for avoiding Ryan Whitmore yet again, something she'd done successfully since she was sixteen years old.

THE GRANDMOTHERLY receptionist listened patiently as Annie explained why she couldn't fill out the information and insurance papers that were required of every patient.

"Just do your best, honey," the reception-ist said, "and I'll squeeze in Lindsey as soon as I can."

"Don't you need to check with the doc-tor?" Annie blurted out before she thought better of it. She'd half expected to be directed to the nearest emergency room, but her goal was to get Dr. Goldstein to evaluate Lindsey's condition, not pass her off to another doctor.

"Believe me, he'll see her," the reception-ist said with a good-natured smile.

Annie nodded and took a seat beside Lindsey, who had her head down, her sleek brown hair falling like a fashionable curtain over her face.

"How are you holding up?" Annie asked.

"Okay," she said tremulously.

Annie squeezed her thin shoulder and filled out the few blanks she could on the forms. She tried to hand the paperwork to Lindsey, hoping the girl might be caught off guard into providing her phone number. Lindsey shook her head. Figuring now was not the time to hassle her, Annie returned the forms to the re-ception desk and settled back to wait.

Noisy twin boys who were probably still in preschool banged around the waiting room, traveling from toy to toy, their attention spans not much longer than a gnat's. Two seats away, a surprisingly calm woman who looked vaguely familiar leaned over. Her thin legs poked out beneath baggy madras shorts, and she wore her frizzy blond hair in a ponytail.

"One of my boys has a little cold, but they're mainly here for a checkup," she said. "I already told the receptionist your Lindsey could go ahead of us."

"Thanks," Annie said.

"You don't remember me, do you?" She placed a bony hand on her chest. "I'm Edie Clark now, but my maiden name is Cristello. We went to high school together."

Now that the other woman had identified herself, Annie wondered how she could have failed to recognize her. Edie had been one of the popular girls who whispered and giggled whenever Annie passed them in the hall.

"We just moved from Virginia after the school year ended. That's where my husband's from. I convinced him Indigo Springs was a great place to raise a family." Edie looked pointedly at Annie. "Do you have kids?"

The door to the inner office opened. A fortyish nurse with a kind face appeared, clipboard in hand, calling out, "Lindsey Thompson."

"Go ahead, Lindsey." Annie nodded to the girl, who got unsteadily to her feet and moved gingerly through the office.

The nurse stood back, letting Lindsey precede her through the inner door, but didn't immediately follow. Her gaze zeroed in on Annie. "Wouldn't you like to come with her?"

Annie couldn't imagine her presence would help put Lindsey at ease. The opposite might be true. "Won't you be there when the doctor examines her?"

"Well, yes," the nurse said.

"Then I'll wait here."

"Very well." The nurse's slow acceptance of her decision made Annie wonder if she'd made the wrong choice. "I'll come get you when the doctor's done. You'll want to hear what he has to say."

Edie gazed at her curiously as the nurse took her leave, no doubt wondering why she hadn't gone with Lindsey. Annie remembered that Edie and her high-school friends had been nicknamed the Gossip Girls long before the TV show became popular.

"Lindsey and I aren't related." Annie decided it would be better to tell Edie the truth than have her spread rumors. "She's a friend of the family."

"I thought she might be a stepdaughter, but I was pretty sure you weren't married," Edie said. "Didn't I hear something about you taking over your father's rafting business?"

"Not true," Annie said, although the misconception was a common one. Some people in town already had her as the new owner. "I'm still a magazine writer. My boss let me take the summer off so I can run the business for my father while he's out of the country."

"He's in Poland, right?" Edie asked.

"Right," Annie said.

One of the twin boys barreled over to Edie, stopped dead in front of her and pointed to his face. Edie dug a tissue out of her purse and wordlessly swiped at the little boy's runny nose.

Annie picked up a magazine on fly fishing and flipped it open. Edie's son rejoined his brother, plopping down on the floor in front of a fort they were constructing from plastic building blocks.

Edie ignored the hint that Annie wasn't up

for any more conversation. "You do know Ryan Whitmore's back in town, right?"

Annie hid a grimace, afraid that Edie and her friends had guessed how Annie felt about him in high school. Why else would Edie bring him up? She composed herself and looked up from the magazine. "Why do you ask?"

Bonnie Raitt started to sing suddenly, her powerful voice cutting off whatever response Edie had been about to give. Annie fished her cell phone from the deep pocket of her shorts, muted the ring tone and checked the display. Her father's number displayed on the small screen.

"Excuse me." She stood up, grateful for an excuse to get away from Edie. She headed for the exit and privacy, waiting until she was outside on the sidewalk to press the receive button. The door of a gift shop next door was slowly swinging shut behind a customer, and she caught the sweet smell of scented candles.

"Hello, Dad." She headed up the hill from the pediatrician's office, away from a group of window-shopping tourists. As the hour neared five o'clock, the traffic on the street had thickened, the number of cars seemingly out of place on the too narrow quaint street. "I've been trying to reach you."

"I didn't have my phone with me." Her father's voice was scratchy and hard to make out, but it was still wonderful to hear from him. After her mother deserted them when Annie was four years old, they'd grown exceptionally close. "Is something wrong?"

"Not really." She got straight to the point. "I called to ask you about Lindsey Thompson."

Interference in the connection combined with the incidental street noise made it difficult to tell whether her father had responded.

"Dad?" Annie prompted. "Are you still there?"

"What about Lindsey Thompson?" His voice sounded odd, but that could have been due to the poor reception.

"She phoned from the train station to say she'd come to visit you. She said she knows you through Joe Nowak."

There was a long pause before he said, "That's true."

"Why didn't you ever tell me Helene Nowak had a daughter?" Annie asked. "I'm positive you didn't mention it when she died."

"I didn't." The strange vibe remained in his voice. "Where is Lindsey now?"

"Here in Indigo Springs. With me. There were no trains back to Pittsburgh today so now I'm wondering what to do with a fifteen-year-old."

"Lindsey told you she was fifteen?"

"Isn't she?"

"She's thirteen," her father said.

Thirteen.

The unlucky number flashed in Annie's mind like a neon warning sign. And just like that, she knew.

Her muscles clenched and her stomach muscles tightened against the blow that was coming. It was the only way the events of the past few hours made sense.

"Who is Lindsey Thompson, Dad?" she prompted, her voice already trembling.

"I didn't want you to find out this way."

She suppressed an urge to toss the cell phone into the street, where the tires of a passing car would smash it. She took a deep breath and smelled exhaust fumes. She forced her vocal chords into action. "Want me to find out what?"

"She's your daughter."

Annie sank onto the nearest stoop. The traffic continued to pass by while across the street a bell jingled as customers went in and out of an ice-cream shop, the scene the same as it had been moments before.

But for Annie, everything had changed with three world-shattering words.

"There you are." Edie Clark appeared as though she'd materialized out of thin air. "I told the receptionist I'd come out and get you."

"Annie?" Her father's voice came over the phone, urgent and worried. "Are you okay?"

She wasn't okay. She'd just discovered the father she'd trusted had let friends adopt her baby, expressly going against her wishes that he arrange a closed adoption. And one of the biggest gossips in Indigo Springs was regarding her with open curiosity. "I can't talk now, Dad. I'll call you back later."

Annie disconnected the call and summoned the will to stand up, determined to appear normal.

"Sorry to interrupt your call," Edie said brightly, "but Ryan's waiting."

She must have misspoken. Annie had gone to the pediatrician specifically to avoid dealing with Ryan Whitmore. "You mean the *pediatrician* is waiting?"

"Oh, no. That's why I asked you about Ryan earlier. His office closes early on Fridays." Edie indicated the placard on the door behind Annie, and she realized they were in front of Whitmore Family Practice.

The office hours that were listed confirmed the office was indeed closed. "Dr. Goldstein had a family emergency, so Ryan's taking his patients this afternoon."

Somehow Annie managed to nod, although her entire body felt numb. She concentrated on placing one foot in front of the other as she followed Edie to the pediatrician's office, bracing herself for the ordeal to come.

But how could she possibly prepare to talk to Ryan Whitmore when the girl they'd conceived when they were both only sixteen had inexplicably resurfaced?

CHAPTER TWO

RYAN WHITMORE leaned one shoulder against the bright-blue wall outside the examination room, making a notation on young Lindsey Thompson's chart.

A pint-sized girl with a mop of dark curls stuck her head around a door frame down the hall from where he stood. She was about four years old. He waved. She giggled, her head disappearing back into the room.

As soon as he talked in private to whomever had brought in Lindsey, it would be the little girl's turn.

The nurse who'd been assisting him came back, walking down the hall with another woman trailing her. Ryan blinked once, then twice, but his eyes weren't wrong.

It didn't matter that the nurse partially obscured his view and a baseball-style cap covered the second woman's hair. He would have recognized her from a hundred feet away, which was about as close as he'd come to her since they were teenagers.

"Dr. Whitmore, this is the woman who brought in Lindsey," the nurse said when they reached him. "Annie—?"

"Sublinski," he finished, keeping his eyes trained on Annie, who had yet to meet his gaze. "We went to high school together."

"Then you don't need me," the nurse said cheerfully. She excused herself as though the chance meeting was nothing out of the ordinary.

She couldn't know he and Annie Sublinski had last spoken more than thirteen years ago on the telephone about giving up the baby she was carrying.

The nurse couldn't possibly be aware of all the things Ryan had never said to Annie, or the guilt that never quite went away no matter how much he tried to live in the moment.

He shook off the memories and focused on the present.

"This is a surprise," he said.

She raised her eyes. The color was an unremarkable mixture of brown and green. He was at a loss as to why he'd always found them so fascinating.

She'd been appealing as a teen but was even

more so now that she was nearly thirty. Her bare arms and legs were toned and tanned, and she had a natural, clear-skinned look that could put a cosmetic company out of business—if not for her port-wine stain. He wondered why she'd never had it removed.

"For me, too." Her eyes were guarded, as though she'd noticed him assessing her birthmark. He hoped she hadn't. "A surprise, I mean. I didn't know you were filling in for Dr. Goldstein."

She clearly wouldn't have brought Lindsey to the pediatrician's office if she had. A few years back, while he was visiting family over Christmas, he'd spotted Annie coming out of Abe's General Store. The downtown had been decorated with wreaths and festive lights, the perfect setting for an apology. Annie had spotted him coming and promptly crossed the street, rushing through the snowflakes drifting from the sky before disappearing into her pickup.

"About Lindsey." She held herself stiffly, like a cornered animal ready to take flight. "Do you know what's wrong with her?"

Now obviously was not the time to bring up the past.

"We can talk in there." He nodded toward

his colleague's office. She hesitated, then complied, not looking at him as she passed. He followed her into the room, closing the door with a soft thud.

She winced at the noise, edged backward and crossed her arms over her chest. Her weight shifted from foot to foot.

Pretending her body language didn't bother him, he hoisted himself up on the edge of the desk that dominated the room. "There's nothing wrong with Lindsey a glass of orange juice and a sandwich won't cure."

"Excuse me?"

He tapped the girl's file against his palm. "Her blood sugar was low. The last time she ate was this morning, and all she had was yogurt."

"That's all that was wrong with her?"

"Like a lot of teenage girls, she has some skewed ideas about how much she should weigh," he said. "We gave her some juice and a granola bar one of the nurses had left over from lunch, but she could use a good meal."

"I should have asked if she'd eaten." Annie seemed to be talking to herself as much as him. "At the train station, I should have asked her."

"The train station?" he repeated.

She nodded. "In Paoli. I picked her up an hour or so ago."

"Who is she?"

Her eyes shifted, which they'd been doing a lot. "A friend of the family."

That didn't compute. Whoever had filled out the forms, and he had to assume that was Annie, hadn't even known the names of Lindsey's parents.

"I don't know much about her," she answered as though she'd read his mind. "I didn't even know she was coming. She's here to visit my father. Her grandfather's a friend of his."

That didn't make sense, either. "Didn't I hear that your father is in Poland?"

"Lindsey didn't know that."

"Shouldn't her parents have known?"

Annie looked away again, heightening his sense that she was hiding something. "I don't think they know she's here."

"Have you called them?"

She seemed to be clenching her teeth. "Kind of tough to do without a phone number."

So that's what Annie was concealing. Now that she'd admitted she didn't have a home phone number for Lindsey, it was easy to piece together what had happened today.

Lindsey had gotten on a train without telling her parents she was leaving, which just might qualify as running away from home. He thought about the little girl who'd waved at him from the room down the hall. She was going to have to wait a little longer for the doctor to arrive.

"Let's go see Lindsey." He hopped down from the desk, yanked open the door, then let Annie precede him. There wasn't much space between him and the door, but she managed to squeeze through without touching him. He caught a whiff of her clean, outdoorsy scent, and he was transported back years, to the single night they'd spent together.

"Second door on the right," he told her, his mind thick with memories. How could that night, which had been so special, have had such shattering repercussions?

She hung back, wordlessly indicating he should enter the room ahead of her. He wasn't as careful to avoid contact as she had been, inadvertently brushing her arm as he passed. She jerked sideways as though pricked by a porcupine.

Damn. He'd found it charming that she'd been flustered around him when they were in high school, but this was a new reaction altogether. She was nervous—and not in a good way.

The hell of it was that he couldn't talk to her about it. Not now. As a doctor, his primary responsibility was to his patient. He had a more pressing matter to deal with than his regrets over the past.

His priorities back in order, he strode through the door to find that Lindsey had moved from the exam table to a chair in the corner of the room. Her color was better, but he read apprehension on her face when she saw Annie following him. What was that about? he wondered.

He smiled at her, an easy task. Lindsey was trying her hardest to act grown-up, but underneath her brave front was a rather charming child. "How's that orange juice going down?"

"I'd rather have a Diet Coke." Her quick comeback and smile reminded him of somebody he couldn't quite place.

"Juice is a better choice," Annie said.

Lindsey's smile faded, her hand tightening on the half-full glass. "I like Diet Coke."

"Annie has a point, Lindsey," Ryan interjected. "You need nutrients to build up your blood sugar, and diet soda won't cut it."

He didn't give Lindsey an opening to respond, pulling a piece of paper from her file and extending it to her. "I need some information for our records before I can release you."

With obvious reluctance, she took the form and the pen he handed her along with it.

"I realize you don't know your insurance information," he added, "but it would help if you filled out what you can."

Lindsey nodded before turning her attention to the form, her brow knitting in concentration as she wrote. Annie stood like a statue just inside the door, keeping as far away from him as possible.

Her low opinion of him smarted, although he didn't blame her. He should have made his peace with her years before now. He could use the excuse that getting through med school and his residency had required total concentration and dedication, but that's all it was: an excuse.

Within moments, Lindsey handed the pen and paper back to him. A quick glance at the form confirmed he'd achieved his objective: The girl had written down her phone number.

"So, can we go?" Lindsey asked.

"As long as you promise to eat something," Ryan said.

Lindsey stood up, although her jeans were so tight he questioned how she could move.

She held up the granola bar, from which she'd taken maybe two bites. "I'm already eating something."

"Something more than a granola bar," Ryan clarified.

"I'll see to it that she has a meal," Annie said.

Lindsey slanted her a dubious look. He wondered if Annie had any experience dealing with teenagers, but then he speculated about a lot where Annie was concerned.

Like whether she'd ever forgive him for that night.

"Bye, Dr. Whitmore," Lindsey said.

"Bye, Lindsey."

The girl strolled out of the examination room. Before Annie could follow, Ryan caught her arm in a gentle grip. She inhaled sharply.

"Let me go." Her voice was an urgent whisper.

Stung, he did as she asked. "I was just going to give you Lindsey's home phone number."

She pursed her lips, mumbling, "Sorry." She fumbled in the pocket of her shorts, withdrawing her cell phone. "What is it?"

He read off the ten digits, which she entered, never once glancing up at him. "Thank you," she said.

"You're welcome."

She started walking away from him, rebuilding the distance she'd kept between them all these years. "Annie?"

He thought she'd pretend she hadn't heard him and keep on walking, but then she turned. "Yes?"

"It was good to finally talk to you again."

He supposed it was too much to hope that she'd echo the sentiment. She nodded once, then pivoted, as though eager to get away from him.

He didn't stop her retreat. Not this time. But now that she was back in his life, he wouldn't let her walk out of it again until he said his long-overdue piece.

ANNIE had never held the baby she delivered.

After a lengthy, tough labor, she'd heard a lusty cry and felt like weeping herself. The nurse had brought the infant close enough for Annie to see her, but she'd only gotten a brief look.

She'd been awed that she had helped create someone so tiny and perfect, but she'd tried to pay attention to the baby's red, wrinkled skin. Anything to take her mind off the enormity of what she was giving up.

Even though her heart was aching, she

hadn't protested when the nurse claimed it was best for the separation to be immediate. From her experience with her own mother, who'd popped in and out of her life before finally disappearing for good, Annie knew the nurse was right.

The nurse had whisked the baby away, and Annie had fully expected never to see her again.

"You're staring at me," Lindsey accused.

Annie blinked, and the snack counter at the back of Abe's General Store came into focus. They were sitting on red vinyl stools, their reflections bouncing back at them from the stainless steel of the old-fashioned soda machine. She smelled grease from the grill and the hot dogs on the rotating rack.

Annie had been taking a mental snapshot of Lindsey that she could call to mind in the years to come. It wouldn't be difficult. The shape of Lindsey's face, the spacing of her eyes, the arch of her eyebrows and the even whiteness of her smile were all reminiscent of Ryan.

Ryan, who brought out the nervous, insecure teenager in her that she'd desperately wanted to believe was gone forever.

She fought the feeling that she'd been unfair in not revealing who Lindsey was. It was better this way. If Ryan never knew

Lindsey was the baby they'd given up for adoption, he wouldn't have to lose her all over again.

The way Annie was going to.

"I can't eat when you're looking at me like that," Lindsey complained.

They'd swung by the snack counter after leaving the pediatrician's office. Annie had given Lindsey a ten-dollar bill, then stepped outside to phone the girl's parents, nervously wondering whether they'd recognize her as Lindsey's birth mother. The call had gone straight to voice mail.

"I'm sorry," Annie said. "I didn't realize I was staring."

"Well, you were." Lindsey set her nibbled-on sandwich back down on her bare plate.

Annie worried that the girl should have ordered something more substantial than turkey on rye bread and a Diet Coke. If the woman who'd prepared the food hadn't left the counter, Annie would ask her to throw in potato salad or at least a bag of chips.

"You should finish that." Annie nodded at the sandwich.

"It's not very good."

Of course it wasn't. It contained no cheese, no pickle, no lettuce, no tomato and probably no condiments. Annie pursed her lips, unsure of what to do or say next. Uncertain how to get a teenager to do anything at all.

"Dr. Whitmore would tell you to eat your food," Annie said, dismayed that she'd resorted to using his name.

Lindsey's mouth twisted, but she picked up her sandwich and took a bite.

Was there already an invisible connection between Ryan and Lindsey? Is that how he'd succeeded in getting the girl's phone number when Annie had failed?

How would he react if he knew the truth? Surely he'd noticed how edgy Annie was, so why hadn't he guessed? A reason occurred to her.

"How old did you tell Dr. Whitmore you were?" she asked.

Lindsey didn't look up from her food. "Fifteen."

Now that Annie knew the truth, it was easy to see through the lie. "Is fifteen how old you need to be to travel alone on the train?"

"I don't know," Lindsey mumbled.

"I think you do know," Annie said. "That's why you said you were fifteen when you're only thirteen."

Lindsey's head jerked up. "How do you know I'm thirteen?"

"My father told me."

Lindsey swiped strands of her long hair out of her face and sat up straighter, an eager light in her eyes. "Is Uncle Frank back? Did you ask him if I could stay?"

Annie's fingers clenched into fists. How could her father not have told her about Lindsey? She'd confided in him when she got pregnant and trusted him to handle the adoption arrangements. Her faith in him had been so absolute that she'd signed the papers severing her parental rights without reading them. She'd never dreamed he'd give her baby to someone Annie might possibly know.

"I talked to him on the phone," Annie said. "He'll be in Poland for at least another month."

Lindsey's head dropped again. "What else did he tell you about me?"

"Not much," Annie said. If she was alone, she'd call her father back and demand answers, the six-hour time difference be damned. "I don't even know what grade you're in."

Or if Lindsey knew she was adopted.

"I'll be in eighth grade in September," Lindsey said. "I'm almost fourteen, you know."

Her birth date was in mid-March, which meant Lindsey wasn't yet thirteen and a half. She wondered if Lindsey had written down her true birthday on the medical form or whether she'd tried to preserve the fiction that she was fifteen.

She also wondered how closely Ryan had looked at the form.

"And you live in Pittsburgh?" Annie asked.

"Not *in* Pittsburgh exactly," Lindsey said. "We live in Fox Chapel. It's near Pittsburgh."

"Any brothers or sisters?"

Lindsey narrowed her eyes. "Are you going to ask my phone number next?"

Annie had been attempting to fill a desperate need to find out more about Lindsey, but that wasn't what the girl had asked. "I already called your parents."

"But…but how did you get the number?"

"The form in Dr. Whitmore's office."

From the shocked expression on Lindsey's face, she hadn't considered that possibility.

"I left your parents a message," Annie continued. "They're probably worried sick about you."

"They don't even know I'm gone," Lindsey said. "Dad took Timmy and Teddy to Kennywood, and Gretchel's working.

She's supposed to pick me up at a friend's house at five o'clock."

Kennywood, Annie knew, was a popular amusement park near Pittsburgh that was one of the oldest in the nation. "Who's Gretchel?"

"My stepmother."

"Are Timmy and Teddy your brothers?" Annie asked.

"Sort of," Lindsey said. "I'm adopted. They're not."

Annie bit her lower lip to find it trembling. Lindsey had been matter-of-fact in stating she was adopted, but she considered Annie's father to be her uncle and not her grandfather. Lindsey obviously didn't know the truth about her birth, and it wasn't Annie's place to tell her.

"That doesn't make them any less your brothers," Annie said.

Lindsey blew air out her nose, but stayed quiet. Neither did it seem as though she planned to eat any more of her sandwich. Yet she needed nourishment. She was too thin and still pale enough that she looked as though she might topple off the stool.

"You could have another dizzy spell if you don't eat," Annie said. "You don't want to go back to the doctor, do you?"

Lindsey's blue eyes flashed. "At least Dr. Whitmore was nice to me. If I came to visit *his* father, he wouldn't make me go back to Pittsburgh."

Her words were like blows. Annie had tried to forget about the daughter she'd given up, but now that she'd met Lindsey she realized how miserably she'd failed. The clawing need to know the girl was as fierce as the unconditional love that nearly overwhelmed her. She couldn't give in to that love without risking that somebody would figure out Lindsey was her birth daughter. If only the girl knew how desperately Annie wanted to keep her around. Annie swallowed, pushing words past the lump in her throat. "It's for your own good."

"Annie Sublinski," a deep male voice announced from behind them. "What brings you off the river?"

Annie swiveled on her stool to see Michael Donahue moving toward them, his tall frame dressed in jeans and a work shirt, his thick, dark hair slightly sweaty. Since moving back to Indigo Springs earlier in the summer, he'd gone into business with the Pollocks, who owned a local construction company.

She'd always felt a certain kinship toward Michael because he'd been another of the outcasts of Indigo Springs High. An incident at this very snack counter had landed him in juvenile detention. Fathers, including hers, had warned their daughters to stay away from him.

He'd since redeemed himself in dramatic fashion, although very few people knew he was the hero who'd rescued a child from drowning during an Indigo River Rafters trip earlier that summer. "Hey, Michael," Annie said, then turned to Lindsey, preparing to introduce her.

"Wait a minute. Don't tell me why you're here. Let me guess." Michael placed three fingers on his forehead and closed his eyes before snapping them open. "It has something to do with a young brunette."

Lindsey giggled at Michael's antics, but Annie's breath caught. Did he know about the child she'd given up for adoption? Could he? Surely there'd been talk when Annie had abruptly left town before her senior year of high school. Had somebody figured out that the real reason she'd moved in with her ailing grandparents was because she was pregnant?

"I'm Michael Donahue." He jumped in with an introduction before Annie could untie her tongue. "And you are?"

"Lindsey Thompson," she supplied. "I came to visit my uncle Frank, but he's in Poland."

"I heard something about that," Michael said. "You took over your dad's business, right, Annie?"

His question stopped Annie from denying her father's relationship to Lindsey. "Actually, I didn't. I'm just filling in while he's gone."

"My bad. Some people in this town like to talk even when they don't know what they're talking about." He spoke from experience, Annie thought. At one point town gossip about him had been rampant. He winked at Lindsey. "Pretty soon they'll be spreading stories about you."

Annie willed her heartbeat to slow down. It had been an innocent remark.

She and Lindsey didn't share a strong resemblance, and Annie was barely old enough to be the mother of a teenager.

"There's nothing to talk about." She forced her voice to sound normal. "Lindsey's a family friend."

Michael pulled open the glass door of the refrigerated unit beside the counter, then paused. "I thought she was your Dad's niece."

"We're not really related," Lindsey interjected before Annie could panic. "I just call him uncle."

Michael nodded, accepting the answer. Some of the pressure inside Annie's chest eased as he removed four bottles of water from the refrigerator.

"We're finishing up a remodel job down the street and the crew is getting thirsty," he explained. "Good seeing you, Annie. And a pleasure meeting you, Miss Lindsey."

"He was nice," Lindsey said as he walked away.

"Most people in Indigo Springs are," Annie said.

Lindsey looked unhappy. "Then why can't I stay here?"

So far three people who'd known Annie as a sixteen-year-old had seen her with Lindsey and none of them had put the pieces together. In all probability, nobody would, ensuring that Lindsey wouldn't have her world inadvertently turned upside down.

"I've been thinking about that," Annie said slowly. "Maybe you don't have to go back just yet."

"You mean I can stay?" Lindsey asked excitedly.

The thought of letting the girl go without spending at least a little time with her was like a dagger through Annie's heart. Staying in

Indigo Springs was clearly what Lindsey wanted, too. Annie simply wasn't strong enough to fight fate and what she so desperately wanted anyway.

"Only if your parents say yes," Annie said.

"They'll say yes." Lindsey smiled and took a big bite of her sandwich, unaware she'd agreed to a visit with her birth mother.

That was exactly the way Annie intended to keep it.

MAYBE SHE'D messed up in coming to Indigo Springs, Lindsey thought.

Uncle Frank had made it sound really cool, but the downtown was nothing but a bunch of old buildings. Once she and Annie had gotten back in her truck and headed out of town, all she'd seen was trees.

The parking lot they'd pulled into wasn't even paved, and the building they were approaching looked like a grungy warehouse. A couple of dozen sturdy-looking bikes were parked in neat rows off to one side. On the other were nine or ten faded picnic tables.

Lindsey read the sign over the door: Indigo River Rafters.

"*This* is your father's business?" she asked Annie.

"This is it," Annie said.

Lindsey slowed down but didn't dare stop. If she did, the gnats that were flying around her hair might attack her eyes. She supposed the setting was okay, although there weren't a lot of trees close to this part of the river and the grass around the shop was trampled down dirt. The water was maybe fifty yards away, with a flatbed trailer blocking part of the view.

"All our trips end here at base camp. That spot over by the flatbed trailer is the take-out point," Annie said. "We load the boats so we can transport them to the put-in for the next trip."

"Boats?" Lindsey asked.

"Rafts, kayaks, tubes." She pointed to a pair of yellow school buses so old you couldn't pay Lindsey to get in them. "We shuttle the customers in those."

Annie acted like it was really important to her that Lindsey like it here, which was totally different from her attitude at the train station. Earlier, Annie's main goal had been sending Lindsey home.

"Can't you just drag a raft down to the river and go?" Lindsey asked, although there was no way she'd do that. The bugs wouldn't be as bad out on the river, but she shuddered just thinking about the mud and the cold water.

"You could," Annie said, "except the river's like a one-way street. It only flows in a single direction."

Whatever, Lindsey thought. That hadn't been what sounded so cool when she'd heard about the business. "Uncle Frank said there was a store."

"It's more like a gift shop," Annie said. "We sell T-shirts, waterproof sandals, sunglasses—that kind of thing. It supplements the income from the river trips and the mountain-bike rentals."

Great, Lindsey thought with a sinking heart. *Just great.*

"Where does your dad live?" Lindsey asked.

Annie pointed to a tiny building behind the shop. "Back there. That's where we're going."

Lindsey stopped walking. "Are you serious?"

"Why wouldn't I be?"

Lindsey thought of the big, five-bedroom, two-story house she'd woken up in that morning. "I guess I just expected something different when Uncle Frank talked about all this."

Lindsey made a face when she spotted

the rocking chairs on the wooden porch, but the inside of the house turned out to be not so bad. A decent-sized room with a really old TV opened into a kitchen. The furniture was simple—a navy blue sofa and wood chairs. Beyond the kitchen was a smaller space with a washer and dryer.

Annie indicated the left side of the house. "There are two bedrooms with separate baths over here. You can sleep in my dad's room."

"Cool," Lindsey said. She could stay here, she decided, which was a good thing because she had nowhere else to go.

"I need to finish up a couple of things at the shop," Annie said. "Will you be okay for an hour or so?"

"Yeah, sure," Lindsey said, but she ran out of things to do after putting her clothes in an empty drawer and checking her e-mail on the computer with an ancient modem.

She was flipping through a magazine from a nearby rack when Annie showed up. No way was she going to read *Field and Stream, Outdoor Life* and *Backpacker.*

"Don't you have anything good?" Lindsey asked. "Like *Vogue* or *Elle*?"

"Afraid not," Annie said.

Lindsey held up an issue of something

called *Outdoor Women*. On the cover was a picture of three women with fishing poles standing in river water up to their thighs, with mountains rising behind them.

"Who reads this lame stuff?" Lindsey wrinkled her nose.

"Enough people to keep me employed," Annie said. Lindsey must have looked puzzled, because Annie added, "I wrote the cover story."

"Get out!" Lindsey eagerly turned the glossy pages until she found the article. It was about something called heli-fishing, where helicopters flew fishermen to remote areas that couldn't be reached any other way. "Oh, my gosh. Your name's on this story. That's really awesome."

"Didn't you just say the magazine was lame?"

"Well, yeah. But getting your name in a magazine is cool." Lindsey rethought her lukewarm opinion of Annie. "Maybe one day you can write about something better."

Annie looked doubtful. "The outdoors is pretty much my thing."

"Not mine." Lindsey rolled her eyes. "I'd take a mall over a river any day."

Annie perched on the edge of the sofa near where Lindsey sat on the floor. "Then why did you come to visit my father? There aren't any malls in Indigo Springs."

Lindsey stuffed the magazines back in the rack. "I didn't know that. I thought there were malls everywhere."

"Is something wrong at home?" Annie seemed to be deciding what to say. "You can tell me if you don't feel…safe."

Lindsey had sat through films in health class about the different types of abuse. She knew what Annie was really asking. Wow. Was she way off!

"There's nothing like that going on," Lindsey said.

Annie seemed to relax. "Something must have happened to make you leave home. Your parents will be calling back soon. It would help if I knew what it was."

Lindsey stood up. "I just needed to get away, that's all."

"Away from what?" Annie asked.

Lindsey waved a hand. "Away from every-thing."

Now that Annie was on board, Lindsey wasn't going to say anything that would get her sent back to Pittsburgh. She was staying put if she could help it.

Anywhere was better than home.

CHAPTER THREE

WELL, that hadn't gone well.

Annie watched helplessly as Lindsey retreated into the bedroom she was using. The girl had changed out of her jeans into a pair of gray jersey knit shorts with *Princess* printed across the bottom.

Princess. Yeah, Annie was way out of her league when it came to Lindsey.

She'd half feared that Lindsey would change her mind about staying and say she wanted to go home, but the girl had surprised her. Not that the visit would be a done deal until she talked to Lindsey's parents.

Annie had left a second message for them and could barely concentrate while she waited for the phone to ring. Sometime between inviting Lindsey to stay and now, Annie had allowed herself to hope for time to get to know the girl.

No. Not hope. That was too mild a word.

She *craved* more time with Lindsey—and she was desperately afraid she wouldn't get it.

The phone rang, making Annie jump. She hurried into the kitchen and picked up the receiver of the wall-mounted phone. "Hello."

"Annie, it's Ryan."

Annie's brain froze, her throat closed up and her legs almost gave out. She could only think of one reason for him to call.

He knew.

She put a hand on the counter to steady herself. Her heart pounded like a jackhammer. She braced herself, struggling to decide whether she would admit the truth.

"I'm calling to see how Lindsey's feeling," Ryan said.

How Lindsey was feeling? His words didn't compute. She'd expected him to say he'd guessed Lindsey was the baby they'd given up for adoption.

"Annie? Are you still there?"

"Yes," she choked out, feeling overwhelming relief. "I'm here."

Her voice sounded raspy and unfamiliar with none of the maturity she'd strived so hard to develop over the years.

"How is Lindsey?" he asked.

A few more seconds passed. She closed

her eyes briefly. She was handling the call poorly, arousing suspicion where there might not be any. She fought to regain her equilibrium. "Fine. She's fine."

"Good to hear. Just make sure she doesn't skip meals and she shouldn't have the problem again."

"Okay. Sure." She still sounded unsophisticated and unsure of herself, which was unacceptable. Especially with Ryan Whitmore on the other end of the line. *Get off the phone,* her brain screamed. *The less you talk to him, the better.* "Thanks for calling."

"Wait!" Ryan's appeal was loud enough that she heard him even though she was just about to hang up. She reluctantly held the phone back up to her ear.

"You're guiding the ten o'clock white-water trip tomorrow morning, right?" he asked.

"I'm planning to," she said slowly, afraid of what he would say next.

"Good, because I'm thinking about taking it."

She grimaced at the prospect of Ryan coming along on one of the trips, invading her world. How could she do her job with him in one of the rafts, reminding her of a past she didn't want to think about?

A beep sounded, signaling an incoming call. Annie normally considered it rude to place one person on hold to talk to another. Rarely, if ever, did she use call waiting. She didn't intend to now, either.

"I've got to take this call," she said. "It could be Lindsey's parents."

"Of course," he said. "I don't mind hold—?"

"Goodbye," she interrupted, pretending not to hear him. She disconnected, then answered the other call. She was right. The caller was Gretchel Thompson, Lindsey's stepmother.

Out of the fire and into the inferno, Annie thought.

"Thanks for calling," she said. "I'm Annie Sublinski, Frank Sublinski's daughter."

"Oh, yes," Gretchel said. "Your father's visited us a bunch of times, usually with Lindsey's grandfather. He's a great guy."

Gretchel seemed to have no idea that Annie was Lindsey's birth mother. Had her husband failed to tell Gretchel about the adoption arrangement? Was it possible he didn't know about it, either?

Annie realized she had something in her hand. It was a piece of paper she'd crumpled into a ball from the pad she kept by the phone. She set it down and explained how Lindsey had ended up in Indigo Springs.

"I'm so sorry," Gretchel said. "I'll have a return ticket waiting tomorrow morning at the train station."

"I wanted to talk to you about that." Annie prayed she wouldn't sound too eager. "Since Lindsey's already here, why not let her stay a while?"

"You want her to stay?" The woman sounded incredulous.

Lindsey wandered into the kitchen and stood against a wall, watching Annie with hooded eyes.

"It'll give me a chance to see why my father is so fond of her." Annie took a breath, trying to figure out how to persuade Lindsey's stepmother to agree to the visit. "I promise to take good care of her."

"Since you're Frank's daughter, I'm sure you would," Gretchel said. "Could I talk to Lindsey, please? I'd like to hear what she has to say."

"Sure." Annie kept her excitement in check, reminding herself Gretchel hadn't agreed to anything yet. She held the phone out to Lindsey. "She wants to talk to you."

Lindsey moved toward Annie as though she were walking the plank. She took the receiver and listened, no doubt to a scolding, in silence. Her face seemed to run the gamut of expressions, from annoyance to acceptance and finally to what Annie hoped was pleasure.

"Yes," Lindsey said. "I want to stay."

The weight that felt as though it had been pressing on Annie's heart lifted. She took the phone from Lindsey, one question paramount in her mind.

"How long can she stay?" Annie asked.

"I'll get back to you on that," Gretchel said. "To be honest, it might be better if Lindsey's out of the house for a while. She's a good girl, but as you'll find out she can be sullen and unhappy. Lately we've had some... friction."

"Anything I should know about?"

"Nothing important," Gretchel said. "Just teenage stuff."

Annie was painfully aware it wasn't her place to ask for the details even if the girl hadn't been listening in on the conversation.

"It's settled, right?" Lindsey asked after Annie hung up. "I can stay?"

"You can stay," Annie confirmed.

Lindsey clapped her hands and smiled. Annie smiled back, enjoying the moment but realizing trouble might lie ahead. Now that she'd cleared one hurdle, a bigger problem remained.

What was she going to do about Ryan?

RYAN had expected Annie to avoid him when he showed up for the Saturday morning white-water trip. He hadn't anticipated she'd be a no-show.

In his experience, the person in charge tended to at least be on-site during the busiest times of the week. Unless, of course, there was a good reason for her to stay away.

Like a man she clearly wished would leave her alone.

Letting Annie dodge him, however, was the one thing his conscience would no longer allow him to do.

He waited until the few dozen rafters who were taking the morning trip had boarded the bus and he was the only one left in the shop before approaching the long-haired kid at the counter.

"When's the next white-water trip?" Ryan asked.

"Two o'clock." The kid didn't bother to point out that Ryan had arrived in plenty of time to take the first one.

Ryan stuck out a hand. "Ryan Whitmore."

Looking suspicious of a customer who introduced himself, the kid took a few moments before he shook Ryan's hand. "Jason Garrity."

"You been working here long, Jason?" Ryan asked.

One of the fans behind the cash register blew a lock of Jason's hair into his eyes. He tucked it behind his ear, his fingers brushing against his gold stud earring. "About a month. You want me to sign you up for the afternoon trip?"

So much for small talk. "That depends on who's guiding the trip."

"It'll probably be Annie," Jason said. "She usually does the morning run but she switched off today."

"When did she do that?" Ryan leaned one of his forearms on the counter as though he was only casually interested in the answer.

"Last night, I think," Jason said. It had probably been right after Ryan had mentioned his interest in the trip. "Jill—she's one of our other guides—showed up here pretty early to take her place."

Ryan glanced at the wooden wall clock, which was shaped like a fish. At shortly past ten, it wasn't early anymore, but the little house behind the shop where Annie lived had looked suspiciously quiet. Lindsey might still be asleep but it didn't make sense that Annie would be. "Do you know where Annie is?"

"Yeah," Jason said. "She took a mountain bike out on the trail."

"Which trail?"

"The one with the view of the river, out past where the cars are parked," he said.

"Any idea when she'll be back?" Ryan asked.

"I don't know." Jason frowned at him. "You sure ask a lot of questions."

"I guess I do," Ryan acknowledged and left it at that. He slapped the counter once with the palm of his hand and headed out the door. "Thanks."

He sat down at one of the outdoor tables outside the shop that were set up for rafters waiting for the trips to leave. He situated himself so he had a view of the bike trail, stretched out his legs and crossed his arms over his chest.

Annie might have avoided having him along on one of her white-water trips, but she couldn't evade him forever. Sooner or later, she'd ride her bike back to the river rafters.

When she did, he'd be waiting.

ANNIE leaned over the handlebars of her mountain bike and pumped her legs, trying to concentrate on climbing the hill.

Unfortunately all she could think about was Ryan.

She'd timed her ride so she wouldn't be back at Indigo River Rafters until after the ten o'clock group left for the river. That way she'd miss Ryan entirely.

Perhaps she was a coward for not facing him, but there was no point in complicating things. Gretchel Thompson hadn't set a date for Lindsey's return, but school started two weeks from Monday. That was sixteen days from now.

Annie was determined to keep the circumstances of Lindsey's birth a secret so the girl's life could return to normal at her visit's end. She already knew hers never would.

Not when the baby she'd given up had grown into a young girl with a face and a name and a penchant for sleeping late.

Annie's lungs strained for air and her breaths came in short gasps as she approached the crest of the hill. Her mind whirled as much as the bike wheels while she tried to come to terms with her decision not to tell Ryan about Lindsey.

She was rotten at keeping secrets and always

had been. Her father maintained that she was the most straightforward person he knew.

Her father.

He'd phoned minutes after she'd awakened, full of apologies for keeping the truth about Lindsey's adoption from her all these years.

His excuse was that he couldn't bear to lose all contact with his granddaughter.

As though it had been his decision to make.

It seemed her father wasn't the only one who'd kept secrets. He reported that the late Helene Nowak had had so much trouble persuading her husband, Ted, to agree to adopt that she hadn't told him she knew the birth family. Lindsey had been told she was adopted but given no further details.

All of which put Annie in the uncomfortable, uncharacteristic position of hiding the truth.

She crested the hill, the burning sensation in her thighs finally easing. The tough part of the ride was over. The rest of the way was downhill, with the dirt trail cutting a path through a thicket of trees and emerging near the field Indigo River Rafters used for a parking lot.

Air whooshed over her face, cooling her

skin and blowing through her hair as the bike jostled over the slightly uneven ground.

She glimpsed base camp in the distance, her signal to ease up. Intending to coast the rest of the way, she stood up, resting her weight on the pedals.

The left pedal snapped off with an audible click.

Annie's foot touched air and then the sole of her shoe scraped along the dirt of the path.

The bicycle skidded sideways, sliding out from under her. She pitched forward, her upper body going airborne. The ground rushed up to meet her.

Desperately fighting the impulse to tense up, she let herself fall. The right side of her body smacked the ground, with her rear end absorbing the brunt of the impact.

Then she was half sliding, half rolling down the hill.

"Annie!" Someone was calling her name. She was too stunned by the fall to figure out who it was.

She smelled grass and saw stars. She blinked a few times and her vision cleared enough for her to realize she was sprawled in a soft patch of grass to the side of the trail.

"Annie!"

She heard the same voice, closer this time and jarringly familiar.

She groaned, not so much in pain but in dread. Sitting up, she struggled to gather her scrambled wits for the confrontation she couldn't avoid.

"Are you okay?" Ryan Whitmore's face entered her field of vision, his handsome features full of concern. He bent over, looking as though he intended to determine the extent of her injuries.

She raised a hand, dismayed to find it shaking. "I'm fine."

"Are you sure?" He didn't touch her but still hovered over her. "That was quite a fall."

She didn't yet know how badly she was hurt, but wasn't about to admit to anything. She brushed the leaves and the grass and the dirt from her arms and legs, taking stock of her injuries. A bad scrape on her right thigh. A sore spot on her hip that would turn into a bruise if it hadn't already. A banged-up elbow.

And severely wounded pride.

"Like I told you," she said, "I'm fine."

Before he could insist on helping her up, she got to her feet. Various body parts screamed in protest. The world went momentarily black, the stars returning before they performed another disappearing act.

"Let me help you down the hill." Ryan's eyebrows were drawn together, and his mouth was pinched. She ignored his outstretched arm.

"You can carry the bike if you want to help." She doubted she'd be able to lift it, not when she'd yet to recover her wits fully. She took a step, relieved when her leg supported her weight. She might be bruised and stiff, but she'd live.

He seemed about to protest, but then crossed the path to where the bike had come to rest against a bush. He righted it, then frowned. "It's missing a pedal."

"That's why I fell," Annie said. "When I stood up and put my weight on it, it came off."

"Odd," Ryan said.

"Not so odd," she said. "Things like that happen."

Too bad it had had to happen while he was watching. Annie trudged ahead of him, silently cursing her bad luck. If she'd stuck to the original plan to guide the early group down-river, she could have at least avoided one-on-one time with him.

"I thought you were going rafting," she said.

"I thought you'd be the guide."

She looked down at the trickle of blood running down her leg instead of at him. The scrape on her thigh smarted so she doubled her efforts to walk as though she was injury-free.

"All our guides are capable," she said.

"Yeah, but only one of them has been avoiding me for almost fourteen years."

She kept walking, determined not to let him know his comment had thrown her, irked that it had. "I haven't been avoiding you. I just haven't had anything to say to you."

"If I was the kind of guy who took advantage of the injured," he said in a conversational tone, "I'd take exception to that comment."

"I'm not injured," she denied.

"I'd disagree with that one, too."

She increased her pace, which should have been enough to put distance between them. She was in hiking shape, and he was rolling a broken bicycle, but the fall had slowed her down. The sun was shining brightly overhead, heating up the August morning and making her feel even more uncomfortable.

"You should let me take a look at you when we get back to your shop," he said as though she hadn't already refused him. "Then there are a couple of things I want to talk to you about."

Before alarm took hold, the rational part of her brain kicked in. He sounded too cool and calm to have figured out the volatile secret about Lindsey.

"You can't always get what you want," she said.

It was a childish retort, one she immediately wished she could take back. She was a grown woman who successfully dealt with men in both her business and personal lives. She'd had a serious romantic relationship, even though it hadn't worked out in the end. It bothered her that she became a quivering mass of nerves in this man's presence.

"You're right," he said. "I learned that lesson when I was sixteen."

He was wrong. He'd gotten exactly what he wanted that night when she'd had sex with him. She'd later found out it was precisely what he'd set out on having.

She felt her face heat and could have kicked herself. She was no longer a teenage virgin. What had happened with Ryan had been a long time ago. She couldn't let it matter. She couldn't let *him* matter.

They'd almost reached the main building. Jason must have seen them approaching because he came outside. He'd changed the black T-shirt he'd worn to work into a green one with the Indigo River Rafters logo. In black jeans and with his sandy hair falling to his shoulders, however, he still looked like he was headed for a rock concert.

"What happened to you?" Jason asked.

"The pedal came off the bike," she said. "Could you put it in the storeroom with the extra rafts? I'd rather the customers didn't see it."

"Sure." Jason took the bike and the broken pedal from Ryan before disappearing around the corner.

Annie turned to face Ryan once they were alone again. He was possibly even more handsome than he'd been in their youth. His hair had darkened slightly so it tended more toward light brown than blond, and there were laugh lines around his eyes and mouth she didn't remember being there.

In khaki shorts and a T-shirt, he looked more like the athlete he used to be than a doctor. His legs were long and leanly muscular, and his arms and chest were nicely developed. His features—sensuous mouth, clear blue eyes, long straight nose—packed a powerful punch. She'd never thought it fair that one man had so much going for him.

"Thanks for your help," she said and headed for home.

"You're really not going to let me check those scrapes?" His voice stopped her progress.

She answered without turning. "I've told you a couple of times now, I'm fine."

"Then I'll check your mountain bikes."

He was suddenly beside her. It had always surprised her that she didn't need to look up far to meet his eyes. She guessed he was five-eleven, tops, but he'd been such an over-whelming figure in her life that he'd always seemed much taller.

"For loose pedals," he added.

The suggestion was an excellent one, considering she'd be liable if a customer had a mishap. They called in a technician to service the bikes regularly to prevent exactly that.

"I'll get Jason to do it," she said.

"I worked in a bike shop one summer. I can help him."

"You don't have—"

"I want to," he interrupted.

She stared at him, at a loss as to what to say to get him to leave. Lindsey was probably awake by now; she could appear at any minute. Common sense dictated that the less time

Ryan spent around the girl, the less chance he'd have to figure out their connection.

"I'll get started on the bikes while you clean up." He strode toward the rack of mountain bikes available for rental, as though she'd already given him permission.

Cursing herself for not speaking up more forcefully against his help, Annie started for the house. Lindsey was sitting on the sofa in front of the television, her legs tucked under her, a spoon poised above a small container of peach yogurt. She glanced at Annie, then did a double take. "Oh, my gosh! What happened?"

"I fell off a bike," Annie said.

Lindsey put down her breakfast and unfolded her legs, scooting forward on the sofa. "Need any help?"

It made Annie feel marginally better that Lindsey offered.

"I got it." Annie walked past her into the kitchen and tore a few sheets from a roll of paper towels. She wet them and mopped up the blood and the dirt the best she could, wincing as she did so.

"That looks like it hurts." Lindsey had followed her into the kitchen, yogurt in hand. She wore a gray-and-pink-striped tank top that ended just above the low, elasticized waistband of her very short gray shorts. "How'd you fall anyway?"

"One of the pedals on my bike came off." Annie reached into the cabinet where her father kept bandages and ointments and withdrew some supplies.

"Don't you rent those things out?"

"Yes."

Lindsey made a face. "I'd be afraid to ride one."

The girl's train of thought, Annie noted, was distressingly similar to Ryan's.

"We're checking the other bikes to make sure it doesn't happen again," Annie said.

"Who's we?"

Annie hesitated, reluctant to tell her Ryan was on the premises. "A teenage boy works for me."

Lindsey ate a spoonful of her yogurt, then dropped the container in the kitchen wastebasket. "You sure you don't need any help?"

She not only thought like Ryan, she sounded like him.

"I'm sure." Annie smoothed a gob of salve over the brush burn on her thigh, then tore open a package containing an oversized bandage. She concentrated on centering it over the scrape.

"See you later," Lindsey called.

Annie's head jerked up in time to see the teen headed for the door on long, bare legs, her flip-flops smacking against the heels of her feet. "Wait! Where are you going?"

"To see if I can help with the bikes," Lindsey tossed the words over her shoulder without breaking stride.

"Wait!" Annie called again, but it was too late. Lindsey was gone.

Annie made short work of dressing the rest of her wounds and charged for the door, only to look down at herself and discover her shorts were ripped and her T-shirt streaked with dirt.

She dashed for her bedroom, pulling the T-shirt over her head as she went, and yanked another shirt and pair of shorts out of her dresser drawers. Moments later, she was rushing out of the house, her sore arms and legs aching.

Laughter carried through the clear summer air, a girlish giggle mingling with the deep vibrations of a man's laugh. She followed the sound around the side of the building to the mountain bikes they rolled out of the storeroom each morning, then stopped.

Ryan was crouched on the ground beside

a bicycle, his hand on one of the pedals as he looked up at Lindsey.

"A squirrel really ran into your bicycle wheel?" Lindsey's voice was filled with both laughter and doubt.

"Yep," Ryan said. "Bounced right off. Lay there for a second, stunned, then scampered away."

"Why would it do that?"

"Why do squirrels do anything? You've seen them run into the path of a car. This was the same kind of thing."

"You didn't fall off the bike or anything?"

"Nope. Just wobbled a little."

Lindsey laughed again, then bent her head toward his. "Why are you wiggling the pedals like that?"

"I'm checking to make sure they're securely fastened to the crank."

"The crank?" Lindsey repeated.

"It's this round thing with the jagged edges." He ran his hand over the part, giving her a visual. "It's pretty easy to check. You just jiggle the pedal from side to side to see if you feel any looseness."

Lindsey moved to another bike, imitating what he'd shown her, first on the right pedal, then the left. "I think this left one's loose."

Ryan joined her at the bike, performing the same check she just had. "You're right. Good job spotting it. You might be a natural at this."

Even from her position twenty feet away, Annie could see the effect of the compliment. Lindsey squatted, like Ryan, but she seemed suddenly taller.

If Lindsey had grown up with Ryan as her father, he could have built up her self-esteem in countless interactions instead of just this one.

How could Annie seize the opportunity to spend time with Lindsey, fully aware it could be the only one she'd ever get, and deny Ryan the same chance? Didn't he have as much right as she did to know the girl, no matter how brief their window of opportunity? And if she didn't reveal to him who Lindsey was, could she live with herself?

Lindsey spotted her first. "You didn't tell me Dr. Whitmore was here, Annie. I'm helping him."

"She catches on quick." Ryan's smile reached his eyes. "Hey, Annie."

She didn't attempt a response as she contemplated what would be the right thing to do.

The fair thing.

The decent thing.

He cocked his head. "Are you okay?"

He probably thought the bike accident had knocked some of her brain cells loose. Considering what she was about to do, maybe it had.

Lindsey was regarding her with the same interest as Ryan, her head angled in exactly the same way so their resemblance was unmistakable.

"Can I talk to you alone, Ryan?" She swallowed. There would be no turning back now. "There's something I need to tell you."

CHAPTER FOUR

SINCE their chance meeting at the pediatrician's office, Ryan had thought of little else besides getting Annie alone to talk. As she led him away from the building that housed the river rafters, he got a notion of how alone they would be.

Annie didn't head toward the wide ripple of river that was the best advertisement for her trips or take the shady, tree-lined bike path where she'd suffered the fall, choosing instead a skinny trail that led into the woods.

"We can't chance anyone overhearing us," she told him as she walked along at a clip faster than he would have thought possible given her recent accident. She brushed aside the dangling leaves from a tree branch, forging ahead.

They'd left Lindsey and Jason with the bicycles and instructions to check the rest of them for loose pedals. Lindsey had been pointing out to Jason where the crank was as they walked away.

"Fine with me," Ryan said.

He guessed she wanted to talk some more about Lindsey's fixation on her weight. After they dispatched that topic, he could bring the conversation around to the past they'd never discussed.

He could tell her how sorry he was.

She stopped abruptly. The path was wider here, with a fallen log just about the right height to sit on. She remained standing, but he got the impression she'd sat on that very log before.

She wasn't wearing a ball cap today. A ray of sunlight beamed down through the trees, striking her shoulder-length hair and turning it even more golden. He remembered how he used to be on the lookout for that blond hair in the halls of their high school, but she'd been as adept at avoiding him before their single night together as she had been afterward.

He waited for her to begin, visually assessing the scrape on her leg and the bruise on her arm. She was probably still smarting, but the injuries didn't look serious. She seemed to be having trouble finding words.

"I know why you wanted to talk to me alone," he said, helping her out.

He could see her throat constrict. "You do?"

"It's about Lindsey, right?"

She nodded, her eyes growing huge.

"I'd keep monitoring her, but I don't see this as a big problem. She's fixated on her weight, but she doesn't seem to have an eating disorder."

"An eating disorder," Annie repeated.

"I didn't see any signs of one, which doesn't mean she's not at risk of developing—"

"Stop," she interrupted, holding up a hand.

"Stop?"

"That's not what I wanted to talk about." Annie's upper teeth chewed her lower lip. She crossed her arms over her chest, hugging herself. He had absolutely no idea what she would say.

"Lindsey's the baby we gave up for adoption."

The words hung in the air between them like the fog that sometimes blanketed the Pocono Mountains.

"I found out yesterday just before I talked to you at the pediatrician's office," she said in a rush. "I should have told you then, but I wasn't used to the idea myself. I'm still not."

His brain whirred, trying to put the pieces

together and not able to make them fit. "Lindsey can't be our baby. She's fifteen."

"She lied about her age so she could travel alone on the train," Annie said. "She turned thirteen in March."

The birthday of the baby they'd given up for adoption had been five months ago. Even though he tried to live in the present, he'd marked the date in some way or another over the past thirteen years, sometimes with alcohol, always with guilt.

He sank onto the log, wrestling with the revelation, still trying to make sense of it. He'd never expected to lay eyes on their baby in his lifetime. "Lindsey really is our daughter?"

"Not *our* daughter," Annie said. "We gave up all rights to her. She's Ted Thompson's daughter."

"I don't understand. I thought it was a closed adoption."

"I thought so too until yesterday." She plucked a leaf from a nearby branch, then crushed it in her palm. "It seems my father let the daughter of one of his friends adopt her. He's been visiting her for years."

"Ted Thompson's wife?" he asked, still feeling as though he was wading through fog.

"His first wife. She died eight years ago of

breast cancer. Lindsey lives with her adoptive father and his second wife."

He digested the information. He'd spent the duration of Annie's pregnancy in a study-abroad program in Spain. Since Annie wouldn't take his calls, his mother had kept him informed of developments. She'd relayed that Annie's father had been tasked with handling the adoption.

"What my father did was unforgivable," Annie said. "You have every right to be angry with him."

"Angry?" Ryan searched inside himself but anger wasn't the emotion coursing through him. "I'm not angry."

"Betrayed, then," she said. "My father had no right to do what he did."

Betrayal wasn't what he was feeling, either. Something bright and buoyant burst inside him, so powerful it felt as though it was warming him from within.

"Your father was wrong," Ryan acknowledged, then spoke what was in his heart, "but I sure am glad he was."

"Excuse me?"

He grasped for the right words to explain. "Haven't you ever passed a girl of the right age and wondered if she could be our baby?"

Until he asked the question, he hadn't consciously acknowledged he'd ever done anything of the sort.

"All the time," she answered slowly.

He felt the corners of his mouth lift. "I accepted a long time ago I'd never know where she was or who she was or whether she was happy. But now…" He shook his head at the improbability of it all. "…now everything has changed."

He rose from the log, eager to get back to river raft headquarters. To get back to their daughter.

Their daughter!

"Let's go." He strode down the path, excitement fueling his steps.

"Wait!" she called. "We have more to talk about."

That was an understatement. They still hadn't discussed his culpability in the night that had changed both of their lives. Once again, however, the present was infinitely more important than the past.

"We'll talk later," he said. "Let's go see Lindsey."

He heard the crunching of leaves and her inhale and exhale, and then her hand wrapped around his arm, startling him into stopping.

It was the first time she'd touched him in years, and the contact felt electric. She dropped her hand almost immediately as though she'd felt it, too.

She gazed up at him, her eyes pleading. "You can't tell Lindsey who we are."

He usually considered a situation from every angle before acting, but he had been so impatient to see their daughter he hadn't thought past this minute. "Doesn't she know she's adopted?"

"She does, but her father and stepmother don't even know I'm her birth mother. Only Lindsey's mother knew and she's dead." Her eyes beseeched him. "Don't you see? Telling her would only confuse things. She has a life that has nothing to do with us. In a couple of weeks, that's what she's going back to."

The idealist in Ryan wanted to protest that the truth was never wrong, but the realist conceded they were discussing a minor. Neither he nor Annie had the right to make decisions for her.

"What do you know about her home life?" he asked.

"She lives in a suburb of Pittsburgh. She has two brothers and a stepmother who says she can be sullen and unhappy. I don't know anything about her father."

"If we tell him we're her birth parents," he ventured, thinking aloud, "he might decide that Lindsey should know, too."

"What if he cuts her trip short instead?" she asked. "These next two weeks could be all the time I ever get to spend with her."

He understood her position even though he didn't fully agree with it. "I won't tell her who I am, but I want to spend time with her, too."

Annie exhaled, her shoulders visibly relaxing. "We can work that out."

But could they?

Ryan didn't speak on the walk back to raft headquarters; a question rattled around in his head. How could a thirty-year-old man legitimately spend time with a teenage girl who nobody besides Annie knew was related to him?

The potential roadblock slid into the background when they came upon Lindsey where they'd left her, examining the bicycles with Jason. Ryan barely afforded the teenage boy a look, his attention completely focused on Lindsey.

She jiggled a pedal, her long hair tucked behind her ears, her lower lip thrust slightly forward as she concentrated. The clock rewound a decade and he realized he could have been gazing at his sister as a teenager. Sierra's hair was darker, but she had the same oval-shaped face and delicate features.

Lindsey looked up. Her eyes weren't green like his sister's, or hazel like Annie's. They were blue like his.

"We didn't find any more broken pedals," Lindsey said, "but some chains are loose and a lot of the tires are low."

Ryan could barely think of anything except Lindsey but found it strange that the rental bikes weren't in better working order.

"This shouldn't happen." Annie tried to make sense of it, too. "We have the bikes serviced regularly. The technician was in last Thursday when I was out of town. Right, Jason?"

Jason rubbed his nose, his eyes looking everywhere but at Annie. "I, uh, forgot to tell you. He's on vacation this month. He gave me the name of another guy we could call."

"What?" Annie exclaimed. "That's not something it's okay to forget."

Jason got to his feet, moving with what Ryan recognized as unaccustomed speed. "I'll call him now."

Annie started after him, but Lindsey jumped to her feet and headed her off. "Can't you cut him a break, Annie? Everybody makes mistakes."

Ryan had long thought he and Annie had made a mistake the night Lindsey was conceived but no longer. It seemed miraculous that they'd created this special, beautiful child.

"I suppose I could let it go just this one time." Annie seemed no more able to resist Lindsey's plea than Ryan would have been.

Lindsey had a few more inches to grow but she was already taller than Annie, he noted. Although she looked more like a Whitmore than a Sublinski, she did have Annie's nose: small and straight with a slight upturn.

"Thanks." Lindsey looked from Annie to Ryan and back again. "Now who's going to tell me what Annie said about me."

Annie's eyes flew to Ryan's, her expression guilty as charged.

"I knew it!" Lindsey said. "I knew you two were talking about me."

Somebody needed to deflect Lindsey's suspicion and fast.

"You got us," he acknowledged. "Annie wondered whether we should cancel our date tonight because you're in town."

Annie's mouth dropped open.

Lindsey's eyes widened. "You two are dating? Wow. I knew Annie thought you were hot, but I never would have guessed."

He quirked an eyebrow, keeping his eyes on Annie's reddening face. "Annie told you I was hot?"

"Of course not," Annie protested.

At the same time, Lindsey answered, "I could just tell by the way she looks at you."

"Then no wonder she asked me out." Ryan waggled his eyebrows at Annie.

"Annie asked you out?" Lindsey repeated. Annie appeared incapable of speech.

"Not exactly," he admitted. "I knew she wanted to go out with me, though, so it's almost the same thing."

"It is *not* the same thing," Annie retorted hotly, her chest heaving in indignation. He felt an unexpected stab of lust that explained the origin of his idea—his attraction to her had survived the past.

Lindsey giggled at their interaction. "Don't cancel your date because of me."

"We're not canceling," Ryan said, then added the kicker. "We're taking you with us."

"WHERE ARE we going?" Lindsey asked excitedly after Ryan invited her on the fictitious date.

The traitor.

If Lindsey had declined the invitation, Annie could have wriggled out of it too. She could barely understand how her carefully orchestrated campaign to avoid Ryan had come to this. As of late on Friday afternoon, she hadn't talked to him in fourteen years and now they had a Saturday-night date.

"It's a surprise," Ryan said.

"I love surprises," Lindsey said. "But are you sure it's okay if I come along? Wouldn't you two rather be alone?"

"Of course it's okay. We'll have lots of time to be alone." Ryan had the audacity to wink at Annie. "We're dating."

"Wait just a minute." Annie raised her index finger. "Since when are we—"

"How about walking me to my car, Annie?" Ryan interrupted.

"But—"

"I know we talked about me going rafting today, but I have some paperwork I really should catch up on." He slung an arm around her shoulders, which surprised her so much she lost her train of thought. He applied gentle pressure, ushering her toward the field with the flattened grass they used as a parking lot. She was stunned into walking with him.

"See you tonight, Lindsey," he called.

"Bye, Dr. Whitmore."

"I'm only Dr. Whitmore during office hours," he said. "Call me Ryan."

"Okay," Lindsey agreed happily. "Bye, Ryan."

He kept moving, the right side of his body touching Annie's left, his heat transferring itself to her. He not only felt wonderful, he smelled fantastic, like shampoo, soap and man. Her bones seemed to melt, her physical reaction to him not much different than it had been in high school. And look where that had landed her. She stiffened.

She was about to tell him to take his arm off her when he dropped it. "Sorry about that. I couldn't let you tell Lindsey we weren't dating."

"We're not dating!"

"As of tonight," he said, "we are."

They reached his car, the flashiest one in the parking lot. It figured that the new young doctor in town would drive a Lexus. He leaned against it, looking cool despite the summer sun that beat down on him, appearing far too pleased with the situation he'd manipulated her into. It was time to set the matter straight.

"I'll go out with you tonight," she began, "but only because I understand the date thing is so you can spend time with Lindsey."

"I appreciate that."

She didn't let his charming smile make her lose focus. "Now you need to be aware that there's a difference between going on a single date and dating."

"I do and what we'll be doing is dating." He frowned. "Unless you're already dating somebody else. Are you?"

"Not now," she said, noting his look of relief. "But that doesn't mean I'll date you."

"Then how can I get to know Lindsey?"

"The same way anybody gets to know anybody," she said. "By being around her."

"Nobody in town except you knows I'm Lindsey's birth father," he said. "It wouldn't look right for me to be around her unless I'm also hanging around you."

She squeezed her eyes shut, wanting to argue that his argument wasn't valid, but she still saw his point. "There has to be some other way."

"There is. We could tell her who we are."

Her eyes snapped open. "No! We've been over this. We can't tell her."

He trained his gaze on her. For once, he

wasn't smiling. "Then what do you say? Will you let me get to know our daughter?"

Her throat hitched. Neither of them could afford to think of Lindsey as their own, not when they'd given her away and would soon have to say goodbye again. "I already told you. She's Ted Thompson's daughter."

"Not while she's in town. While she's in town, she's ours. If, that is, you'll share her with me." His voice was low and beseeching, his handsome features strained. Annie had hardened her heart against him long ago but felt the outer layer softening.

"Okay," she said softly, knowing she'd regret the answer but unable to give another, acknowledging that a part of her had anticipated this would happen when she'd told him who Lindsey was. His eyes crinkled at the corners, the way they had all those years ago when he'd lied and told her he cared about her. Even though he hadn't mentioned her birthmark, it felt as though it was searing her cheek.

"See you tonight," he said. "I'll pick you and Lindsey up at eight."

He unlocked the Lexus with his remote, pulled open the door and hopped inside.

Within moments, he'd started the ignition and pulled away.

She stared after him, furious at herself for reacting to him.

She reminded herself she was no longer a sixteen-year-old girl thrilled that one of the most popular boys in school was paying attention to her. She was a poised, self-confident woman who'd recovered from the blow of finding out the truth about their night together.

She'd go along with Ryan's fiction that they were dating, but she intended to set down some ground rules.

He'd hurt her once.

She was determined it wouldn't happen again.

THE TELEVISION in the family room of the gracious old house where Ryan had grown up drowned out his footsteps as he moved over the parquet floor, approaching the Queen Anne sofa from behind.

His sister, Sierra, sat with her back propped against the sofa cushions, her right leg, encased in a ski-boot-style cast, resting on a cherry coffee table.

She dabbed at her eyes with a tissue, then put the tissue to her nose and blew. On the television, a bright blue animated fish was swimming along with a smaller orange-and-white-striped fish in an idyllic-looking sea.

"Are you crying over *Finding Nemo?*" he asked.

Sierra's head whipped around, guilt written plainly on features that instantly reminded him of Lindsey. She plucked the remote from the coffee table and clicked a button, causing the screen to go blank.

She wiped the tears from under her eyes. "I was not crying."

"You were," Ryan accused. "Who would have thought I'd find the Frost Queen bawling over a cartoon?"

"It's an animated movie," she said, "and don't call me the Frost Queen. I don't like it any better now than I did in high school."

He sat on the arm of the sofa, enjoying this glimpse of his usually unflappable sister. "I'll stop if you admit you were bawling."

She glared at him. "A few tears is not bawling. And if you tell anyone, I'll have to hurt you."

"I should tell everybody. It'd soften your image."

"My image is fine just the way it is," she said. "Where have you been all day anyway?"

He let her get away with changing the subject, even though he disagreed with her self-assessment. Word around the office was that she was exceptionally bright but abrupt in her personal interactions, both with patients and staff. She wasn't any different with Ryan. Although only sixteen months separated them, they'd never been close.

"At the office catching up on paperwork," he said, reluctant to share the news about Lindsey.

He doubted Sierra, who'd been a freshman at Dartmouth the year Ryan studied in Spain, even knew Annie had been pregnant. Their mother had been adamant that nobody find out, and Ryan certainly hadn't told her.

"Until seven o'clock?"

"I ran some errands, too," he said.

She didn't ask what sort of errands, probably because she wasn't interested enough to find out. Ryan had moved back into their childhood home six weeks ago after Sierra had badly broken her right leg in a car accident. Most of the time they acted like polite strangers. It might have been different had their parents been present, but their mother had moved into a retirement community after their father's death two years ago.

Ryan stood up, reached into the bowl on

the coffee table and tossed some popcorn into his mouth. "What are you doing tonight?"

"Chad's coming over and cooking dinner for me."

Chad Armstrong was Sierra's long-time boyfriend. A pharmacist at a local drugstore, Chad was a nice enough guy but didn't say much. Scratch that. A mime could outperform Chad in a debate.

"You can join us if you want." The offer sounded more obligatory than sincere.

"I can't," he said, glad he had a reason to refuse. "I have a date with Annie Sublinski."

He wondered why he'd told her that. Sierra was back at the office on a limited basis so she probably would have heard eventually. He doubted she would have asked, though.

"Wow. Really? Did she ask you out?"

"I asked her," he said. "Why would you ask that anyway?"

"Because of the huge crush she had on you in high school."

That couldn't be true. Annie had hardly said a word to him until the night he'd driven her home from one of the graduation parties that sprouted up every June like the yellow wildflowers over the mountainsides. He'd been watching her closely so had spotted her ducking out of the party after a classmate had made a drunken pass at her.

He'd followed, afraid another guy would try to take advantage of her. Once he realized she meant to walk home, he'd jumped into his car and caught up to her a short distance from the party. After she'd agreed to his offer of a ride, nothing about the evening went the way he thought it would.

Before they'd driven a mile, he'd relayed the entire embarrassing story of why he was spending his senior year in Spain. "It's all in the numbers," he remembered saying. "Three varsity letters. Two Cs. Two Ds. And an F."

Annie had listened to his plan to forgo his senior year at Indigo Springs High for twelve months in a study-abroad program. She'd agreed with his parents about the need to prove he was serious about academics. She hadn't laughed when he confessed the prospect of flying across the ocean made him nervous. She'd told him some secrets of her own, most notably about the mother who hadn't cared enough to stay in her life.

Even all these years later, he remembered how comfortable he'd felt with her and how naturally their conversation had flowed.

When he suggested they get out of the car

at a secluded spot and spread the blanket he kept in the trunk, his intention had been to gaze at the starry sky and keep up the amazing conversation.

Then he'd kissed her, she'd kissed him back and neither one of them had called a stop to their lovemaking even though they didn't have a condom.

He'd left for Spain the next morning but had called her the moment he got there. She'd blown him off, mumbling something about a mistake even though it had been way too early to know she was pregnant.

"Annie didn't have a crush on me," Ryan said.

Sierra looked skeptical, but displayed the practicality that was one of her trademarks. "There's a simple way to find out. Ask her."

She lifted her cast off the coffee table and rose slowly to her feet. "If I'm going to be ready when Chad gets here, I need to start now."

She hobbled off, leaving Ryan reassessing his version of what had happened that night. Could Annie really have had a crush on him? If she had, did that make what he'd done even less forgivable?

Knowing he wouldn't rest until he found out, he decided that he *would* ask her.

CHAPTER FIVE

ON SATURDAY NIGHT Annie carefully eyed the windmill with its rotating arms, getting the timing down, waiting for the moment to strike.

She swung back her putter and sent the golf ball shooting toward what should have been an opening between the between the slots.

The opening closed.

The ball careened off one of the gaily painted arms and rolled back to where she stood on the turf at the start of the hole.

"Wow," Ryan said. "I thought I was bad at miniature golf, but you've got me beat."

Annie made a face at him. She wished she could blame the elbow she'd injured in the bike accident, but it was only a little sore. Her more bothersome injury was the scrape on her thigh, but only because she'd needed to wear a skirt so the material wouldn't rub against her skin.

"You really think you're better than Annie?"

Lindsey asked him. "How about when you almost beaned that little kid on the fourth hole?"

Ryan waved a hand in dismissal. "Could have happened to anybody."

Annie had kept quiet long enough. "*We* were on the third hole at the time," she pointed out.

They were now midway through the eighteen-hole miniature golf course, sharing the experience with a crowd largely consisting of tourists. The establishment had opened earlier that summer and had quickly become a popular nighttime gathering place.

Annie hit the golf ball again with the same result. The third time was a charm with the ball finally sliding through the narrow tunnel that led to the hole.

Lindsey was up next. She managed to send her ball through on the first try. Ryan never did accomplish it, finally opting to putt his ball around the apparatus.

"That's three strokes for me, six for Annie and six for Ryan, but only because six is the limit." Lindsey wrote down their tallies on the scorecard with a tiny pencil while they waited for the group ahead of them to finish the next hole. "The way you two are racking up strokes, I'm embarrassed to be out here with you."

"We're not that bad," Ryan protested.

"Not that bad? You're horrible!" Lindsey rolled her eyes dramatically, but she was smiling. "Especially you, Ryan. Aren't doctors supposed to be good at golf?"

"It's not my game," Ryan said.

"I can't imagine you being good at any games," she said with a laugh.

Annie waited for Ryan to stick up for himself, but he just laughed. "He was a three-sport athlete in high school," she heard herself say.

Lindsey bounced her pink golf ball on the pavement and snagged it in mid-air. "Really? Which sports?"

Now that Annie had started defending him, she could hardly stop. "Football, basketball and baseball."

"Get out!" Lindsey said. To Ryan, she asked, "Is that true?"

"It's true."

"But how did you know that, Annie?" Lindsey asked. "Didn't you and Ryan just start dating?"

Annie had expected to feel uncomfortable around Ryan but Lindsey had kept up a running commentary since Ryan had picked them up, mitigating the awkwardness. Now it came rushing back.

"We knew each other in high school," Annie said.

Lindsey practically squealed. "You mean you were high-school sweethearts?"

"No." Annie touched the left side of her face, careful not to look at Ryan. "It means we knew each other in high school."

Annie regretted saying anything at all about their shared past. She searched for another subject, but needn't have bothered.

"Look, there's Jason." Lindsey pointed to the periphery of the course, where Jason Garrity leaned against a fence that overlooked the golfers. "I'm going to say hi."

She dashed off as fast as her skinny jeans would allow her, waving gaily to Jason. When she reached him she tossed her long hair and laid a hand on his arm, the smile never leaving her lips. Jason smiled back.

"If he touches her, I might have to hurt him," Ryan said under his breath. "Does he know how old she is?"

"He'll know soon," Annie said. "You can count on that."

Lindsey laughed at something Jason said

and rested one hand on her hip, like she was posing.

"It can't be soon enough." Ryan sounded as though he was gritting his teeth.

"What are you two doing here?"

Annie stifled a groan at the instantly recognizable female voice. She plastered on a smile and turned to see Edie Clark approaching, her curiosity so evident the word could have been inscribed in red ink on her forehead.

"Same as you, I imagine, Edie," Annie said. "We're golfing."

Edie's eyebrows took on twin shapes worthy of the Arc de Triomphe. "I had the impression you hadn't seen each other in years."

"We hadn't," Annie said.

"So do tell." Edie seemed oblivious to Annie's attempt to dissuade her from further questions. "Who asked who out?"

"I asked her," Ryan said. "I had a thing for her in high school. Found out I still do."

Edie's jaw went slack and her eyes bugged out. Annie cringed. If Ryan had been within elbowing range, he would have gotten a sharp one to the ribs.

"That's…" Edie seemed to be searching for a word. "…sweet."

"Mom! Your turn!" A girl of about seven

with braided dark hair and freckles yelled from two holes away. Edie's twin boys were on their bellies, dragging their hands in a stream of water that ran down the right side of the hole. A harried-looking man was trying to get them to stand up. Edie hadn't moved.

"Mo-om!" The little girl yelled again.

"I've got to go," Edie said with obvious reluctance. "You two have fun."

Edie left them to return to her family, sneaking glances over her shoulder. Edie took her golf club from her daughter but didn't immediately take her turn, instead crossing to her husband and saying something to him. Her husband turned and looked at them.

"Did you have to tell her you had a thing for me in high school?" Annie kept a smile on her face, acting as if nothing was wrong. "It's not even true."

"Yeah, it is."

Annie wasn't interested in his lies. "She'll tell everyone she knows what you said."

He shrugged his broad shoulders. "So what?"

"So she's a gossip." She winced at the volume of her voice. She deliberately lowered it and moved a step closer to him, loathe for anyone to overhear. "What do you think she'll make of it when she sees Lindsey with us? What if she figures it out?"

"How could she figure it out?" he asked. "It's not like you had a crush on me in high school."

Her stomach rolled.

"You didn't, did you?"

She'd been careful during their long-ago night together not to let him find out. She lowered her eyes, wishing her honest streak wasn't so wide. "I don't have a crush on you now."

A burst of childish laughter rang out, followed by a golfer's shout that he'd made a hole-in-one, but the silence between Annie and Ryan seemed deafening.

"I don't understand. Then why did you blow me off when I called you from Spain?" He moved closer, lowered his voice even more. "It was before you knew you were pregnant."

A part of her wanted to hurt him the way she'd been wounded. "Maybe the fantasy was better than the reality."

He winced as though she'd struck him.

"Hey, you two! You're holding everybody up." Lindsey hurried toward them, gesturing that the hole they'd been waiting to play was free. "Lowest score goes first so I've got honors. Again."

Annie was so aware of the change in Ryan that she could barely keep her mind on her golf game. He was quieter, more contemplative, no doubt because of her childish, cruel comment.

She had no luck putting through the front door of the little red schoolhouse, onto the right lane of the metal bridge or into the clown's mouth. By the time they reached the eighteenth hole, she couldn't stand it any longer. While Lindsey was lining up a putt, considering it from every angle, Annie edged over to Ryan's side.

"I'm sorry," she said. "I shouldn't have said that."

"Why not? You meant it, didn't you?" He didn't wait for an answer, inclining his head in the direction of Edie and her family. "Edie's been watching us all night."

She blinked up at him, surprised by the abrupt change of subjects. "I noticed."

"I've been thinking about it," he said, "and unless we act like a couple, people might wonder why we're together."

"I don't under—"

He kissed her before she could finish her sentence, just leaned down and captured her mouth. His lips felt warm and soft, and he smelled…intoxicating. Like his kiss.

His mouth moved over hers, his lips tasting and teasing, coaxing her into forgetting the very valid reasons she shouldn't be kissing him. Remembered sensations swamped her so that she couldn't distinguish between the past and the present. They blended together, creating one perfect moment.

One perfect kiss.

Somebody whooped.

Ryan's lips clung to hers a moment longer, then he lifted his head and smiled into her eyes.

"Did you see that putt?" Lindsey called, swinging her head around. Annie's brain wasn't fast enough to signal her feet to move. Lindsey caught them not quite in the act.

Lindsey smiled knowingly. "If you're not too busy, Annie, it's your turn."

Annie hit her golf ball, dismayed that she could still feel the imprint of Ryan's mouth on hers. She was angry at him for kissing her, but livid at herself for reacting to him.

It had taken her years to recover her self-confidence from what he'd done, time in which she'd grown up enough to learn to protect herself.

Even though one day she might be able to

forgive him, she knew better than to fall for a man who'd slept with her to win a bet with his buddies.

COULD HE be a bigger jerk?

Ryan doubted it. After Annie's comment about the fantasy of who she'd thought he was in high school being better than the reality, he'd handed her a reason to believe he hadn't changed.

He couldn't say for sure what had possessed him to kiss her but it didn't have much to do with gossipy Edie Clark. Maybe it was because he'd sensed the chemistry between them was still combustible and wanted to prove that it at least lived up to the imagination.

It was no consolation that he'd been right.

Now he had something else to apologize for, if he could get Annie to start talking to him again. She hadn't said a word since they'd left the miniature golf course, not that the car had been filled with silence.

"How can you stand not having a mall nearby?" Lindsey didn't wait for either Ryan or Annie to answer. "I think they should be the cornerstone of every civilization."

Ryan briefly removed his attention from

the winding road to glance at the silent Annie, hoping to share an amused look. She kept her gaze averted, but she was struggling to hide a smile.

"You know what else every town should have?" Lindsey asked.

"A mascot?" Ryan answered, even though he was pretty sure it had been a rhetorical question. "When I was a kid, there was a hiker who claimed he saw Big Foot." The local newspaper had written a story about it, although Ryan had never been sure why. "Do you remember that, Annie?"

She could hardly refuse to answer a direct question with Lindsey in the car.

"Who could forget him? The hiker got lost in the woods and said Big Foot showed him the way out." Her smile broke free, which he chose to take as an encouraging sign.

"No way!" Lindsey exclaimed. "Did that really happen?"

"The hiker claimed it did. He said Big Foot had gotten a bad rap," Ryan said. "Sounds like a good candidate for an Indigo Springs mascot to me."

Lindsey giggled. "Not a mascot, a shoe megastore. I think every town should have one of those. Just wall-to-wall shoes."

"Would the sizes go up high enough to fit Big Foot?" Ryan asked.

"You don't really believe in that stuff, do you?" Lindsey asked.

"I believe in possibilities." Ryan slanted another look at Annie, who still wouldn't meet his eyes. "So I'm not ruling it out."

Oblivious to the tension, Lindsey continued her steady stream of conversation until Ryan stopped the Lexus at the river-rafting compound. He accompanied them into the house as though it was expected, determined to talk to Annie alone before the evening ended.

He got help from an unexpected source when Lindsey yawned and stretched her arms overhead. "I'm going to my room."

"So soon?" Annie asked sharply. "Why don't you hang out with us for a little while?"

"Thanks but no thanks." Lindsey was already backing toward the bedroom at the rear of the one-story house. "I'm gonna crash. Maybe listen to my iPod for a while."

Lindsey kept retreating, increasing the distance between them until their trio became a duo. "I'll put on my headphones. It'll be like I'm not even in the house."

She ducked into the bedroom and shut the

door, cutting off the additional protest Ryan felt sure Annie would have made.

"What did she mean by that?" Annie muttered.

Ryan thought it was obvious. "I'd say she wanted to give us time alone."

"What?"

"She was worried she'd be in the way when I asked her to come along tonight, remember?"

Annie marched toward the closed door of the room, showing no signs that the bike accident that morning had slowed her down, her fist already raised. Ryan cut off her path at an angle. "What are you doing?"

Annie either had to stop or run into him. She stopped. No surprise there. "I'm going to tell her she won't be in the way."

He shook his head. "Not a good idea."

"What do you mean—"

He raised a finger to his lips and nodded toward the closed door. Annie fell silent, getting his point. He motioned with his head again, indicating they should relocate to the porch.

"Lindsey thinks we're dating," Ryan said once were outside in the night air. "It'll seem odd to her if we don't spend time alone."

Annie nodded as though she understood.

"Go ahead and go," she said, proving that

she didn't. "I'll stay out here for a while so Lindsey doesn't know you're gone."

"She'll hear the car engine," he said.

"Not if she has her earphones on," Annie argued.

"A lot of times teenagers say one thing and do another."

She apparently couldn't come up with a counterpoint, because she plopped down on one of the twin rocking chairs. The barest sliver of moon prevented him from seeing the nearby river but he could hear the distant murmur of white water. Annie's face was cast half in shadows, the glow from the porch light enabling him to see her displeasure.

The hell of it was, he couldn't blame her.

"I'm sorry," he said.

Her chin lifted, her eyes meeting his. The flare of attraction he'd lit when he kissed her ignited, reminding him of the secondary reason for his apology.

"Not for kissing you," he quickly clarified. He wasn't about to act contrite for being attracted to her. "For kissing you *when* I did. What you said hurt my ego, but I know why you said it."

"You do?" She seemed skeptical.

He sat down on the second rocking chair,

repositioning it so he faced her. Her hands gripped the arms of her rocker as though at any moment she might propel herself out of it and into the house.

"I never apologized for getting you pregnant," he said. "I should have had a condom that night. I should have stopped myself before we went too far."

"I don't want to talk about it," Annie said tightly. "There isn't any purpose in rehashing the past."

That was usually Ryan's philosophy, but that had changed when he saw Annie again.

"In this case, I don't agree." He leaned toward her, his legs slightly spread, his hands resting on his knees. It was a casual position, but he felt anything but relaxed. She stiffened, but he kept talking, the words that he'd kept inside for so long spilling from him. "I should have found a way to come back to Indigo Springs to help you make the decision about what to do about our baby. I should have been there for you when Lindsey was born."

She'd been staring down at the porch, but now her head rose, her eyes meeting his. "If you felt so bad, why didn't you tell me any of this before?"

Her question threw him. "You wouldn't take my calls. I was off at college and then at med school. When we were in town at the same time, you made a point of avoiding me."

"If you'd knocked on my door," she said, "I would have answered."

He fell silent, stifling the urge to argue that she would have slammed the door in his face. Even if that were true, she was right. He had no excuse for not seeking her out except that he hadn't been ready for the responsibility of a baby or the repercussions of giving up that baby. And those were no excuses at all.

"I wasn't fair to you," he said. "I can see that now."

"It's over and done with. Neither of us can change what happened."

He ran a hand over his lower face, not liking the truths she'd forced him to face. A particularly harsh fact was that a part of him had been relieved when she'd decided to give the baby up for adoption. It hardly mattered that he'd make different choices if he had to do it all over again. What counted was what he'd done.

"I don't even know what happened to you when you left Indigo Springs." He knew only that she'd departed before her pregnancy became visible. She was long gone when he returned to Indigo Springs from studying in Spain. "I don't know where you finished high school or how you got the job at *Outdoor Women*."

Even in the semidarkness, he could see her eyes narrow. "Why do you want to know?"

He could think of a dozen reasons but provided the most obvious. "You *are* the mother of my child."

"Ted Thompson's child," she replied.

He wanted to disagree but acknowledged that her way of thinking about Lindsey was healthier than his. She showed no inclination to fill him in on her past so he tried a direct question. "Where did you spend senior year?"

After a moment, she said, "I didn't have a senior year. I got my GED instead."

Fresh guilt spiraled through him. He nearly apologized again for not trying harder to track her down, if only to extend his support. "You did pretty well for yourself. You write for *Outdoor Women*, don't you?"

"Yes."

He'd picked up a copy once at a newsstand and read one of her stories, about snow-machine racing. She had a style that was almost lyrical, making the reader feel the blowing snow and the thrilling exhilaration of competition. "I imagine a staff-writing job for a national magazine is hard to come by. How'd that happen?"

She seemed to be deciding how much to tell him. "I started out as an editorial assistant, but kept pitching story ideas. I finally got the green light to write one. They liked how it turned out, then let me do more. Eventually I got promoted."

He could hear in her story all the things she didn't include. Her determination to get ahead. Her willingness to pay her dues. Her pride in her accomplishment. The shy girl he'd gone to high school with had grown into an amazing woman he didn't know enough about.

"Where's the magazine based?" he asked.

"Erie." The other end of the state.

"Is that where you had Lindsey?"

"Yes," she said.

"Do you still live in Erie?"

"I live in Indigo Springs about a month of the year," she said. "The rest of the time, I go where the stories are."

He thought about how different her life would have been had she kept the baby. "I guess that'll change now that you're taking over your father's business."

"I'm not taking over his business," Annie denied. "I don't know why everybody thinks that. I'm going back to *Outdoor Women* as soon as my dad gets back from Poland."

"Back to living out of a suitcase, you mean," he said. "Sounds rough."

"It suits me." She fidgeted, causing the chair to rock. "Let's talk about tomorrow."

"There's still more—"

"It might be tough for you to spend time with Lindsey," she interrupted. "I'll be guiding trips for most of the day. I'm going to try to get Lindsey to come along, but if she won't she'll probably help in the shop."

She clearly intended the subject of their past to be closed, even though it felt as if there was so much more to say. With difficulty, he thought ahead to the future.

"I have plans until late in the day," he said.

She didn't comment. Since they'd come outside on the porch, she hadn't shown any curiosity about his life at all.

"Why did you tell me about Lindsey?" He asked the question that had been rattling around in his mind since that morning.

The crescent moon disappeared behind a cloud, leaving the porch lamp the only illumination in the dark night. Her face was turned away from the light, her expression impossible to read.

"You had a right to know," she said softly, "and I didn't have the right to keep it from you."

She stood up, walking to the front door and pausing with her hand on the knob. "I think we've spent enough time alone. Good night, Ryan."

He sat there on the porch for long moments after she went inside the house, thinking about how her answer reflected her honesty and integrity. She was a person of substance, someone he'd like to get to know better even if not for Lindsey.

It bothered him that he'd given her good reason, both in the past and tonight, not to feel the same about him.

CHAPTER SIX

ANNIE usually enjoyed being out on the river, with the splash of the white water cooling her sun-warmed skin and the beauty of the outdoors clearing her head.

On Sunday, working the trips had been an ordeal.

She'd designated another guide as the lead so she could bring up the rear, which usually involved nonstop action helping rafters who got stuck on the rocks break free. Both groups were surprisingly competent, giving her too much time to think about Ryan's apology of the night before.

Why hadn't it included the bet? He'd blamed himself for the past and the present—although saying he was sorry for bad timing in kissing her hardly qualified as an apology—but had ignored the humiliation he'd dealt her.

He must not know she'd found out about

the wager, she concluded. Not that she should let it matter now, fourteen years later. Except it did, enough that she hadn't risked resurrecting the pain of his betrayal by bringing up the subject herself.

Because of Lindsey, she'd be forced to get used to having him around. Annie could handle that as long as she didn't do something stupid, like allow him to kiss her again. She couldn't let him into her heart, where she'd already made a place for Lindsey.

Lindsey, whose refusal to take either of today's white-water trips could have had something to do with Jason.

Lindsey walked alongside him while he helped Annie lug the paddles that had been used on the last rafting trip to the storage room.

"Like I told you before, I'll be here at least a week," Lindsey said brightly. Her hands were free, all her attention focused on Jason. Annie felt stupid for not considering Lindsey's ulterior motive for spending the day in the shop until now. "So you'll be seeing a lot of me."

Annie could already see too much of Lindsey. The girl wore tennis shoes with pink laces, a clingy pale-pink T-shirt and a pair of very short white shorts.

She might be too thin but she had curves.

She probably already wore a bigger bra size than Annie.

Jason shook the long hair from eyes Annie had overheard a female teenage customer describe as *dreamy* and said, "Cool."

How could Annie have been so preoccupied with her reaction to Ryan that she'd neglected to have that talk with Jason about Lindsey? She set down the paddles in the storeroom, then motioned to him. "I need to see you in the shop."

"We're not done yet," he said.

"This can't wait," she said. "Lindsey, can you put away some of the paddles for me?"

"Okay," Lindsey said, but she didn't sound enthusiastic.

Jason grinned at Lindsey. "Be right back."

Annie marched inside the empty store, on the door of which they'd already posted a closed sign, and waited for Jason to catch up to her. He'd started out the day wearing an Indigo River Rafters T-shirt but had changed somewhere along the line to his traditional black.

"What's up?" he asked.

"You're eighteen, right, Jason?"

"Yeah."

"How old do you think Lindsey is?"

He shrugged and pushed his long, wavy

hair out of his eyes. "I don't know. Sixteen? Seventeen?"

"Thirteen."

"No way! Wow! That's wild."

"Thirteen, Jason," Annie repeated. "Need I say more?"

Jason put his hands up. "Got it. Stay away from the thirteen-year-old."

Annie could suddenly breathe easier. "Exactly. Lindsey and I can finish putting away the paddles so you're free to go. You're off the next two days, right?"

Mondays and Tuesdays were generally the two slowest days of the week. "Right," he said. "See you Wednesday."

He banged out the front door, letting it slam shut behind him. Annie made a mental note to adjust the hinges, then turned back in the direction of the storage room.

Lindsey stood just inside the door, tension radiating from her. "I can't believe you just did that! How could you?"

Annie swallowed and composed an answer. "All I did was tell him how old you are."

"You told him to stay away from me!"

"Because you're thirteen."

"He wouldn't have known that if you hadn't said anything!"

"He needed to know."

"Why? It's just a number. Everybody says I act way older." She clenched her small hands into fists and thrust her lower lip forward like a petulant child who wasn't getting her way.

"You're not older. You're thirteen." Annie started to say Lindsey was still a kid but thought better of it. She tried another tactic. "I told your stepmother I'd take good care of you. That's what I'm trying to do."

"You're just like her!" Lindsey retorted. "I thought you were different, but you're not."

She pivoted on her pink-laced tennis shoe and stormed away. Annie pressed her lips together.

She should have made sure Lindsey wasn't in the vicinity when she confronted Jason. Failing that, she should have refrained from trying to reason with Lindsey—that had just given the girl more ammunition to argue with.

And now there was a very real possibility Lindsey would ask to cut the trip short. Lindsey's stomach formed a knot. She couldn't let that happen. Neither did she have a clue how to prevent it.

RYAN SANK into the swivel chair outside the exam room and scribbled a prescription, the first chance he'd had to sit down since arriving at the health center in Philadelphia early Sunday morning.

The sights and sounds were familiar from the year he'd spent working at the inner-city Philadelphia location, with a pawn shop and a coin Laundromat in the same block: the cramped space, the patients without health insurance jamming the waiting room, the bright-yellow walls, the cheerful chatter, the friendly staff.

"I still don't know what you're doing here, Ryan." Joy Markham, his favorite nurse, halted beside his chair. She was a grandmother in her early sixties with a no-nonsense attitude and gray hair she defiantly refused to dye. "I thought you were in the Poconos helping out your sister."

"One of the other volunteers cancelled," he said, "so I'm filling in."

She shook her head. "You have got to get yourself a life. I've never once heard you turn down an extra shift and now you're stepping in for volunteers. You don't work here anymore and they're still calling you. Why do you suppose that is?"

"Because I'm thirty years old and single?"

"You're gonna keep on being single if you

don't stop working so much," she sassed. "Do you even have a girlfriend?"

He thought of Annie. "Sort of."

"Sort of? Does that mean you're having trouble convincing some woman what a great guy you are?"

He started. "You think I'm a great guy?"

"Who doesn't?" she said. "Some patients will wait an hour or more to see you, and you know how people hate to wait."

"I didn't know that," Ryan said.

"'Course you didn't. Shouldn't have told you now. We don't want you getting a big head." She rested a hand on an ample hip. "So tell me about this sort-of girlfriend. What's the problem?"

Annie's opinion of him was the problem. Ryan usually didn't get into his personal life in the office, but what would be the harm in getting Joy's take on the situation?

"She doesn't think very highly of me," he said.

Joy's eyes bugged out, wordlessly asking him to continue.

"We went to high school together," he explained.

"So you're saying you used to be kind of a jerk?" Trust Joy to get to the point.

"Yeah." It didn't escape Ryan's notice that *jerk* was the same word he'd applied to himself after he kissed Annie at the miniature gold course. "That's what I'm saying."

"Well, then, that's an easy enough fix."

"It is?"

"You're not a jerk anymore. Anybody who spends time with you is gonna figure that out."

"I'm not following you, Joy."

"Stop working so much and make time for her," Joy said. "You're a doll for coming in today, but you call her right now and tell her you'll see her tonight."

He saluted her. "Aye, aye, captain."

She pointed a finger at him. "Just do it. And another thing. It wouldn't hurt to bring her a little something."

"Flowers?"

"Damn straight. You can never go wrong with flowers."

Luck was on Ryan's side. The patient load at the health center was lighter than usual, enabling him to depart ahead of schedule. He left a message on Annie's answering machine that he'd come by later, then stopped at a grocery store and picked out a colorful bouquet.

He resisted the urge to stomp down on the

accelerator, keeping his speed just above the limit until he left the interstate for the back roads that led to Indigo Springs.

He was rounding a bend on one of the hairpin turns common in the mountains when he caught a flash of movement in his peripheral vision.

It was a dog, loping alongside the shoulder of the road, its tongue lolling. Ryan had barely missed hitting the animal, who might not be so lucky with the next car to come along.

Ryan brought the car to a stop along the shoulder of a relatively straight stretch of road. He checked his rearview mirror. The dog was still coming.

He opened the driver's door and got out. The dog picked up its pace, running toward him, its tail wagging. Ryan could tell it was a puppy from the way it moved and the size of its paws. A mutt, probably part collie, part beagle and part a breed that grew really large.

"What are you doing out here all alone?" Ryan bent down to pet the dog. It wore no tags. Grass, leaves and bits of sticks were caught in its fur.

They were miles from a residential neighborhood. Had some bastard abandoned the dog to fend for itself?

The most sensible course of action would be to drop off the dog at the nearest animal shelter, except the only one he knew of was twenty miles away. It was nearly six o'clock. If the shelter was open on Sunday, it wouldn't be by the time he got there.

The alternative was to take the dog back to his sister's house, relegating the rest of the evening to feeding him, bathing him and getting him settled for the night.

The dog looked up at him, its big eyes full of trust.

Ryan sighed because there was only one decision he could make. He opened the back door on the passenger side, glad he was driving his own car instead of his sister's Lexus.

He couldn't follow his nurse friend's advice tonight. He'd have to call Annie back and tell her he couldn't make it after all.

"Get in, Hobo," he said. "It looks like you just ruined my evening."

ANNIE would make a terrible mother.

Good mothers did not propose after-dinner trips into town for ice cream to a teenager who had behaved badly, not to mention barely touched her dinner, yet that's exactly what Annie had done.

Annie could have argued the trip to the ice-cream parlor was a ploy to get Lindsey to take in more calories, but that wasn't the main reason. She was desperate to smooth things over so the girl didn't leave town early.

"How's that raspberry flavor?" Annie asked.

Lindsey had ordered low-fat frozen custard in a baby cone, which was the smallest portion available.

"Okay," she said.

They'd opted not to eat their frozen treats inside the parlor, or at least that's what Annie had chosen. She'd envisioned Lindsey sitting sullenly across from her and had suggested they stroll down Main Street.

The street was fairly busy for a Sunday night in August, with the tourists who made Indigo Springs a popular summer destination ducking in and out of the bars and restaurants that had been renovated with careful attention to historical detail. Only a few tourists availed themselves of the perfect night for a stroll in the town that seemed stuck in a time that had already passed.

A couple with two young boys passed them, giving Annie a conversation starter. "How old are your brothers, Lindsey?"

"Five and six," she answered without looking at Annie.

Annie did some quick mental calculations. Lindsey's father must have remarried and gotten his new wife pregnant fairly soon after his first wife died. She wondered how that had affected Lindsey, but didn't ask. A question like that could shut down their lines of communication completely.

"I bet things are never boring at your house," Annie said.

"It's a zoo," Lindsey said. "My brothers run wild."

"Then you must be a big help with them."

Lindsey snorted. "Yeah, right."

"Don't you babysit?"

"My parents never ask me to," Lindsey said.

"Then who watches your brothers when your mom and dad go out?"

"Nobody," she said. "They take Teddy and Timmy with them everywhere."

Annie wondered if Lindsey's brothers were a sensitive subject. She licked her ice cream but hardly tasted it, concluding that Annie's chat with Jason was just as likely the source of Lindsey's short answers.

They crossed a side street and entered a

block with single-family row houses inter-
spersed among the gift shops and the florist.

"Don't you just love these stone facades?"
Annie asked. "I hear this block looks pretty
much the same as it did one hundred and fifty
years ago."

She sounded like a tour guide showing off
the city. Lindsey polished off her baby cone,
affording the architecturally significant
buildings only a cursory glance. Annie let
the tidbit about the city getting its start as a
transportation hub for the once-booming coal
industry die on her lips.

She finished her ice cream in quick order
and threw her napkin in a decorative black
metal trash can. The silence between them
grew so pronounced Annie could hear her
own breathing and the soft sounds her flat-
heeled sandals made on the pavement. Her
hip ached where she'd fallen on it.

"Who lives there?" Lindsey finally broke
the silence, pointing up the side street they
were crossing to a large, well-kept Victo-
rian house beautifully situated on a
spacious lawn.

"Quincy Coleman and his wife," Annie
replied, although she stopped short of sharing
the drama that had swirled around Quincy

earlier that summer. "He used to be president of the local bank, but he's retired now."

Lindsey clammed up again. Now that she'd showed interest in a subject, however, Annie wasn't about to let it go.

"Years ago all the fine old families of Indigo Springs lived in this neighborhood," Annie said. "The mayor, the owner of Abe's General Store, lawyers, doctors."

"How about Ryan's family?" Lindsey asked.

"His sister lives about a block and a half up that street." Annie indicated the cross street they'd just passed.

"She's the one who broke her leg, right? Isn't Ryan staying with her?"

"I believe he is."

"Ryan said he'd drop by today. Wonder why he didn't." Now that the subject was Ryan Whitmore, Lindsey was a regular chatterbox.

"He left a message that he'd gotten hung up." Annie had been relieved, not up to dealing with his overwhelming presence. "Something about bringing home a dog."

"A dog! Let's go see it!" Lindsey did a complete one-eighty, heading back in the direction leading to the Whitmore house.

"That's not a good idea," Annie called, hurrying to catch up to her, her hip aching a little more. Her heart started to race. "We can't just barge in on him, Lindsey."

"Why not?" Lindsey asked airily. "He'll be glad to see us."

Annie could hardly dispute that point. She anxiously rummaged for another reason to stay away. "It's impolite to show up without calling first."

Lindsey whipped out her cell phone and started pressing buttons. "He said I could call him anytime," Lindsey said and put the phone to her ear. He must have answered on the first ring. "Ryan? This is Lindsey. Is it okay if we stop by to see your dog?"

Annie was so sure of the answer he'd give, her stomach sank.

"Great," Lindsey said. "We're almost there now."

She pocketed the cell phone, then gave Annie a smug look. "He said it's no problem."

The large, pale-yellow house where the Whitmores had lived for a generation came into view. It had a steeply pitched, irregular roofline and an asymmetrical beauty. The house was notable enough that years ago the local newspaper had written a story about it, describing it as a vivid example of Queen Anne architecture.

"The most romantic house in Indigo Springs," the newspaper had called it. An appropriate backdrop for a boy who Annie thought had grown into the most handsome man in town.

He stood in the front yard with his enviable posture, the soft summer breeze rustling his short, thick hair, holding a leash attached to the collar of a large yellowish-brown dog. An unwelcome spurt of attraction pulled at Annie. There was something irresistible about a man with a dog, something she was determined to resist.

"Come say hello to Hobo," he called cheerfully.

Lindsey didn't need a second invitation. She rushed over to the dog, getting down on her knees to pet him. Annie was slower in arriving, reminding herself Lindsey thought she and Ryan were dating, vowing not to feel uncomfortable around him.

"He's such a cutie!" Lindsey cried. "But I thought you said he was a puppy."

"Hobo is a puppy," he said. "An awfully big puppy."

"That's an interesting name for a dog." Annie deliberately joined the conversation. "Why'd you pick that?"

"He looked like a hobo before his bath," Ryan said. "I found him along the road a couple miles outside of town. I'm pretty sure somebody dumped him."

So he was the kind of guy who not only braked for stray animals, he brought them home. Annie wished he wasn't.

"How could somebody do that to a cutie like you?" Lindsey spoke directly to Hobo. The dog licked Lindsey on the cheek, and she giggled. "I think he likes me. Can I walk him to the end of the block and back?"

Ryan handed her the leash. "My guess is he'll walk you."

The dog took off as soon as Lindsey took hold. She followed, half running, fully giggling.

"Watch out for cars," Annie called after her. Lindsey didn't answer, which wasn't a surprise.

"Maybe she'd like me better if I got her a dog," Annie murmured, realizing too late she'd said the words aloud.

"Tough day?" Ryan asked.

She could have shrugged off the question but he was regarding her as though he truly wanted to hear about it. The burden of shouldering the problem alone suddenly seemed too heavy. She checked to make sure Lindsey was far enough down the street before saying anything.

"Lindsey overheard me tell Jason she was thirteen years old." Now that Annie had started to confide in Ryan, she found she wanted to tell him everything. "She's hardly said a word to me since."

"Had to be done," he said gently. "Give her a little time, and she'll come around."

"I've been afraid she'll say she wants to go home. Even if she doesn't, I don't want to spend what little time we have left together in silence." She gritted her teeth. "Get a load of this. I tried to bribe her into talking to me again with ice cream."

"Did it work?"

"Are you kidding?" She rolled her eyes. "The way to Lindsey's heart is not through her skinny stomach."

He laughed. "I hear you. Food isn't the answer, but a dog might do the trick. She's really taken to Hobo. If you meant what you said about getting her a dog, you can have him."

"Are you serious?"

"It's the perfect solution. Sierra hasn't seen him yet but she's not wild about animals. If I take him to an animal shelter, chances are nobody will adopt him. So what do you say?"

Her inclination was to say yes. She made herself think through the ramifications. "It could work while Lindsey's in town, but not after she leaves. I'm away too much to have a dog and my dad might not want him."

"That's a problem for another day," he said.

A bark sounded. Hobo bounded toward them from a distance, Lindsey trailing him. Her face was split in a huge grin as she ran to keep up with the dog.

"You tell her," Ryan said before Hobo pulled Lindsey the rest of the way into the yard.

"Isn't Hobo the best?" Enthusiasm bubbled from Lindsey. "If you need any help with him, Ryan, I'm your girl."

Annie caught Ryan's eye. He gave her a tiny nod, urging her to take full credit for making Lindsey a very happy girl.

"I talked Ryan into letting us take him home with us," Annie said.

"Are you serious?" Lindsey sounded like she was afraid to believe it. "You'd really let me have a dog in your house?"

"If you want him," Annie asked.

"Yes!" Lindsey shouted, throwing her arms around Annie's neck and hugging tight. "You're the best, Annie."

Annie's eyes teared up as she savored the

hug and the fruity smell of Lindsey's shampoo. The girl let go far too soon. She added an additional thanks to Ryan, then transferred her attention to the dog, showering him with affection.

Annie blinked to clear her eyes. Ryan winked at her. In that moment, she felt like hugging him, too.

CHAPTER SEVEN

ANNIE HESITATED halfway to the reception desk of the Whitmore Family Practice on Monday afternoon when she saw who waited for her, then kept going. Turning back now would only make the next time they met more awkward.

"Hello, Annie. It's nice to see you again," Sierra Whitmore said in the overly solicitous way she'd been greeting Annie since high school.

Annie felt as though she was looking at Sierra through new eyes. With her long, straight brown hair pulled back from her face, a hairstyle that emphasized her high cheekbones and delicate features, the other woman bore a striking resemblance to Lindsey. Sierra had a coolness, however, that was absent in Lindsey.

"Hi, Sierra." Annie didn't add that it was good to see her. It never was. No matter how many years went by, running into Sierra made her relive one of the most agonizing moments of her life.

It had been the day after she'd made love with Ryan, mere hours after he'd left for Spain. Annie had been in town running errands, still savoring the experience. She'd been both hopeful and naive, believing she and Ryan had started something that could survive a long separation.

Then Sierra had tentatively approached her on the sidewalk outside the bank, her eyebrows drawn together as though she wasn't sure she was doing the right thing. Annie still remembered every word Sierra had spoken.

"I'm sorry to be the one to tell you this, but you really need to know." That's all the warning Sierra had provided before delivering the devastating news. "Some guys at school bet to see who can get you to sleep with them first."

The rest of the encounter was hazy, but Sierra had tried to console her, saying something about how immature the boys were. She'd told Annie she knew it hurt, but that it was better she find out sooner rather than later.

Sierra hadn't known it was already too late.

Annie's impulse to touch her port-wine stain was so strong, she clutched at her thigh with her left hand. No need to remind Sierra the birthmark was there, although she could hardly miss it.

"I was sorry to hear about your accident," Annie said.

"Thank you." Sierra's speech was as stilted as Annie's. "I can't be on my feet for long so I'm helping out any way I can."

"I'm sure your patients are glad you're here in any capacity."

"I don't know about that," Sierra said. "Ryan's very popular."

Annie wasn't sure how to respond. She could comprehend how patients would prefer Ryan's warmth, but there was a lot to be said about a doctor who exuded Sierra's cool competence.

Sierra checked the book in front of her, then raised her eyes. "I don't see you in the appointment book."

Hadn't Ryan told his sister he and Annie were dating?

"I'm here to see Ryan on personal business," Annie said. "He has some things for Hobo we didn't take with us yesterday."

"We?" Sierra asked.

"A friend of the family is visiting." *Your niece,* she thought. "A teenage girl. She's watching Ryan's dog for him while she's in town."

Annie felt her muscles tense as she waited for Sierra's reaction. She'd long ago concluded Sierra hadn't been aware Annie had already slept with Ryan when she'd told her about the bet, but she was Ryan's sister. She could know about Lindsey now.

Sierra nodded, apparently unphased by the mention of Lindsey. Annie relaxed but only slightly.

"Ryan's with a patient. If you take a seat, I'll let him know you're here," Sierra said. Annie only got two steps away when she heard her name. "Annie?"

She turned to find Sierra gazing at her with an odd expression. She heard the other woman clear her throat, which was even stranger; Sierra usually oozed confidence.

"Yes?" Annie prodded.

"I know you use another doctor, but I hope you'll reconsider. I can promise that we'll treat you well here."

"Thanks," Annie said, at a loss how else to respond. She wondered if Sierra's offer had been motivated by the past, if the other woman realized how much her "warning" had affected Annie's life.

Annie settled down to wait in one of the vinyl chairs in the reception room. She picked up the nearest magazine, which happened to cover fashion and thought of Lindsey while she flipped through it. The girl had been unremittingly cheerful last night after they'd brought Hobo home, the argument over Jason forgotten.

Ryan appeared ten minutes later, filling up the room with his energy. He was dressed in the same casual manner as at the pediatrician's office, in navy slacks and a blue long-sleeved polo shirt that made his eyes look even bluer.

"Sorry to keep you waiting, ladies." He addressed both Annie and a woman nearby obviously suffering from a cold. "We're a little backed up today, Mrs. Martinelli, but I promise it won't be much longer. Just hold on."

"I'm trying," she said, and seemed to settle more comfortably into her chair to wait.

He caught Annie's eye and inclined his head toward the exit. She got the silent message, standing up and walking with him to the door.

"Hey, Annie," he said in a low voice, his smile reaching the eyes that looked so much like Lindsey's.

"Hi," she whispered back.

Something had changed between them. They were still two people thrown together because they had a treasured teenager in common, but now it felt as though they were a team.

That was a good thing. It was in their best interests to get along, to make the most of their brief time with Lindsey.

"The rest of Hobo's stuff is in my car." He jiggled the keys in his hand and held the door open for her.

The bright August sunshine seemed to bathe Main Street in light, causing the scene outside the office to come alive. It was approaching midday so traffic was heavier than normal, both on the streets and the sidewalk. The town seemed to emit a bright cheerfulness, or maybe that was Annie's mood.

"I'm parked over here," he said. Even though she knew he was in a rush, he didn't hurry. "How'd it go last night? Did Hobo keep you awake?"

"Lindsey slept on the sofa beside his crate. When I woke up this morning, she was asleep with Hobo curled up against her. I think they fell in love at first sight."

"Hobo has excellent taste," he said. They

shared a smile, and again Annie had the sense that they were a unit.

"I already called the animal shelter," he added. "Nobody's looking for Hobo, so the next step is to take him to the vet."

"Already have an appointment for later today."

"Tell the vet I'll be by later to pay for it." He unlocked his car remotely, then reached inside, emerging with a bright-blue plastic water bowl and a teething toy. "This should do it."

"Thanks," she said.

"I can at least finance him," he said. "After all, I'm the one who picked him up off the side of the road."

"I don't mean thanks for that, although I do appreciate it," she said. "I mean thanks for helping me smooth things over with Lindsey. It meant a lot that you let me take the credit for Hobo."

"You're welcome."

She liked having him on her side, she realized. While she doubted the two of them could become close friends after all that had happened between them, they could certainly be friendly.

"You're coming over tonight, right?" she asked.

"I'll be there," he said. "What time's good for you?"

"Is seven-thirty too late?" she asked. "I have some paperwork I need to finish up."

"Perfect. It'll give me a chance to get in a workout," he said. "How about if I bring a pizza?"

"Sounds good," she said.

He handed her the dog supplies, his hand inadvertently brushing hers. "See you tonight."

"Tonight," she repeated.

He turned and waved before disappearing into the office. She rubbed her hand, recognizing the thrill that had shot up her arm as physical attraction.

So what if it was?

She was too smart to get involved with him a second time.

Besides, what could happen with Lindsey acting as a chaperone?

RYAN CAUGHT the inbound pass, weighed his options, drove to the basket and went up for a score. Another body came hurtling across the court, leaping at him with a hand outstretched to block the shot. The basketball reversed direction, bouncing off Ryan's head and out of bounds.

"That's what I call a headbanger!" Chase Bradford shouted.

Ryan rubbed the top of his head and located Johnny Pollock on the outdoor court, which wasn't tough to do. Monday was usually a slow night for pickup basketball, and there were only four of them present. Added to that, Johnny wore black safety goggles because he'd been poked in the eye last week.

"Hey, Pollock," Ryan called. "You should have warned me Chase was obnoxious."

"What can I say?" Johnny was bent over, breathing hard, his hands resting on his thighs. "That's just his personality."

"Come on!" Chase protested. Ryan had heard he was a forest ranger. He looked the part—tall and fit with sun-lightened hair and tanned skin. "You told me to get in his head."

"Damn, Chase," Johnny complained. "Tell him our strategy, why don't you?"

"Just keep taking it to 'em, Ryan." Michael Donahue, Ryan's teammate in the two-on-two game, returned from retrieving the ball from some nearby bushes to stand on the sideline. Like Johnny, he'd been a few years behind Ryan at Indigo Springs High. "They're afraid of you."

"He's missing all his shots," Johnny said. "Why should we be afraid of him?"

"You gonna take that?" ·Michael asked before tossing the ball to Ryan.

He caught it, squared up to the basket and launched a three-pointer that felt good coming off his fingertips. He raised his hands in the air in triumph before the ball swished through the hoop with perfect backspin.

"Lucky shot!" Chase yelled.

Ryan scored again on a pretty defensive move the next trip down the court, then followed it up by dishing the ball to Michael for the winning layup.

"That's it!" Chase declared as the four of them gathered at the bench on the side of the court where they'd left their water bottles. "I'm done with the trash-talking."

"Good idea." Ryan picked up his water bottle and drank thirstily. "You suck at it."

"Tell me about it," Chase said. "Everything about my game's rusty. I need to play more."

"Chase was a single dad for a while." Johnny was sitting down on the bench, his legs spread in front of him. "Now his girl-friend helps out with his son."

"Fiancée," Chase corrected. "We're getting married later this year, then we're going to legally adopt Toby. Kelly's already a great mom."

"Congratulations." Ryan thought there was probably a story there. "I'd like to meet her sometime."

"How about tomorrow night?" Michael's face was damp from where he'd splashed water on it. "A group of us are getting together at the Blue Haven. You and Annie should come."

"How do you know I'm seeing Annie?" Ryan asked.

"Sara told me." Sara Brenneman was Michael's girlfriend and a lawyer with an office a few doors down from Whitmore Family Practice. "She hears everything so she knows everything."

"Then she knows about the teenage girl visiting Annie." Ryan figured it was best to talk about Lindsey openly as though he had nothing to hide.

"Only because I told her," Michael said. "Her name's Lindsey, right? Nice kid. I met her the other day with Annie."

"Annie won't want to leave her alone."

"Does Lindsey babysit?" Chase asked. "I'd rather not ask my dad. He and his wife are settling into their new house."

"Charlie and Teresa got married!" Michael exclaimed, while Ryan figured out that the Charlie Bradford who'd been in for a physical last month was Chase's father. "When did that happen?"

"My dad talked Teresa into flying to Las Vegas last weekend," Chase said. "He didn't want to give her a chance to change her mind about marrying him."

"Sounds like something Charlie would do," Michael said, chuckling. "So you and Kelly didn't go to the wedding?"

"Hell, yes, he did." Johnny joined the conversation, answering for Chase. "Kelly got my wife to agree to watch their little boy, then told Chase no way were they missing the big event."

"She can be a bossy little thing," Chase said as if he minded, but he sounded like a man in love.

Ryan wished there was a woman who cared enough about him to make sure he did the right thing. His mind skipped to Annie and the night they had planned. He tossed his water bottle in the trash just as he spotted another player approaching the court. "Here comes a fourth. I need to call it a night anyway."

He headed away from the men, fishing his

cell phone out of his bag, intending to order a pizza, then take a quick shower.

"Ask Lindsey about the babysitting," Chase's voice trailed him. "I'll call to see if it's a go."

"Sounds good," Ryan responded casually, as though getting together at the Blue Haven wasn't a big deal. On the surface, it wasn't. Couples met friends in bars every night of the week.

Except this *was* different because he and Annie weren't a couple in the traditional sense. Sometime in the past few days, though, he'd gradually realized he wanted them to be.

Joy had suggested he spend more time with Annie. If she agreed to the Blue Haven, she might start wanting to be with him instead of feeling it was a duty.

Those, however, were very big ifs.

THE DOG leaped in a blur of yellowish-brown fur. Ryan stood his ground, holding the cardboard takeout box above his head while withstanding the assault of oversized puppy paws scratching at his legs.

"Down, boy," he said.

The dog's eyes were bright, his tongue

hanging from a mouth that looked as if it was grinning. Ryan laughed aloud and reached into his pocket, withdrawing the rawhide bone he'd picked up at the drugstore and giving it to the eager dog.

"Bad boy, Hobo!" Lindsey appeared, pulling the dog away from the door by his collar so Ryan had a path to enter. She slanted Ryan a narrow-eyed look. "Did you just reward him?"

Ryan felt like a little boy caught scarfing down cookies before dinner. "I guess I wasn't supposed to do that?"

"No, you weren't. I need to train him not to jump on people. If he's anything like Angel, it's gonna be, like, so hard."

Considering she'd stopped scolding Hobo and was hugging his neck, Ryan silently agreed she could have a tough road ahead. "Is Angel your family's dog?"

"She was my dog." The expression on her face suddenly looked too serious for someone so young. "I got her after my mom died."

Sympathy stabbed at him, not only for Lindsey's loss but for the woman who'd mothered her through the first years of her life. "What happened to Angel?"

"I had to give her away." Lindsey's voice cracked. "My brother Timmy has allergies."

Ryan heard the resentment in her voice and couldn't fault her. Giving up her beloved dog must have brought the pain of losing her mother back. He wondered why Lindsey's family hadn't pursued other options, such as buying a doghouse or enclosing the back porch.

"I'm sorry," Ryan said.

Lindsey nodded, her eyes meeting his.

"If you get tough on Hobo, you won't have trouble training him," Ryan continued in a lighter voice. "The way he looks at you, you could have him doing anything you say."

"I hope so."

He walked through the great room to the kitchen, setting the pizza box down on the table. His stomach rumbled at the spicy smell of sauce and cheese. "Where's Annie?"

"Changing clothes. She had a busy day." Lindsey had followed him into the kitchen. Her straight hair fell to the middle of her back. In blue jean shorts and a short-sleeved red top dotted with tiny hearts, she reminded him of the way his sister Sierra had looked as a teen.

He pulled out a chair from the kitchen table and sat down. "How about you? Did you have a busy day, too?"

"Pretty busy." Lindsey opened and closed

kitchen cabinet doors as she talked. "We got Hobo his shots at the vet, and I've been trying to housebreak him. He's going to spend a lot of time at the shop, so I'm shop-breaking him, too."

Finally finding what she was looking for, she pulled some paper plates and napkins from a cabinet and carried them to the table. Hobo followed closely behind her, clamoring for attention. Ryan bent down to pet the dog.

"What's that on your arm?" Lindsey asked as she set down the dishes.

Ryan glanced down at the long, angry-looking scratch he'd already treated with antiseptic. "A war wound from the pickup basketball court. I play after work a couple times a week."

"I didn't know guys your age still played basketball."

"Hey!"

She giggled as she crossed to the refrigerator, pulled out an unopened large bottle of diet cola and poured herself a glass. Lindsey, who seemed to have talked Annie into buying her drink of choice, had been teasing him.

"In between wheezes, one of the guys

asked if I knew a teenager who could mow his lawn," he said. "So I recommended you."

She whirled. "You did not!"

He winked at her. "You're right, I didn't. But I did say I'd ask if you could babysit."

He heard a door opening and the soft thump of footsteps. Even with his attention divided between Annie's approach and Lindsey, he still noticed the wariness that descended over the teenager.

"How old is the baby?" she asked.

"Thirteen months, I think."

Annie entered the kitchen, wearing a Save the Planet T-shirt and khaki shorts that didn't entirely cover the healing scrape on her thigh. Her legs and feet were bare and her hair tumbled to her shoulders, free of her usual ponytail. She looked beautiful. He felt himself smile. "Hi, Annie."

"Hi." This time, she smiled back. "Who has a thirteen-month-old baby?"

"Chase Bradford," Ryan said.

"I know Chase. His fiancée Kelly, too. They're a nice couple." Annie opened the cardboard pizza box. "This smells great. Thanks for picking it up. You even got pepperoni."

"Pepperoni's a must. Without it, it's only a pizza-like substance." He waited while the two females helped themselves, Annie to a regular-sized piece and Lindsey to the smallest one in the box. "Chase asked if Lindsey could babysit tomorrow night."

"Do you want to babysit, Lindsey?" Annie asked.

Lindsey paused in the act of picking off the pepperoni from her pizza. Too fattening, Ryan guessed. "If they'd trust me with the baby, sure."

"Why wouldn't they trust you?" Ryan asked.

"I've never even babysat my brothers."

"I'll vouch for you," Ryan said. "Look how trustworthy you are with Hobo."

Annie pulled two beer bottles from her refrigerator, the dark, rich color marking the brew as his favorite brand of Irish stout. She held one bottle up to him with a questioning look. He nodded, then he could have kissed her when she got two chilled mugs from the freezer.

It seemed as though she shared an affinity for one of his favorite things.

"Wednesday, tomorrow night," Annie repeated slowly. "We don't have anything else planned."

"I've been meaning to talk to you about that," Ryan said. "Chase and Kelly are getting together with some friends at the Blue Haven. I'm pretty sure you know the other couples—Penelope and Johnny Pollock, and Michael Donahue and Sara Brenneman. They invited us to come."

Annie had a piece of pizza in her hand. She set it back down on the plate. "They know we're dating?"

"Word travels fast," he said.

"Did you tell them we can't make it?" Annie asked.

"Why can't you make it?" The question came from Lindsey. "If I babysit, you don't have to worry about me." She gasped and covered her mouth. "But if nobody's home, who'll take care of Hobo?"

"It'll only be for a couple of hours," Ryan said. "Hobo needs to get used to staying by himself."

The dog whimpered, walked in a circle then started to lift its leg. Lindsey bolted out of her chair.

"No, Hobo! Not in the house." She pulled the dog by his collar, herding him toward the door, pausing only long enough to attach a leash.

Annie waited until Lindsey was out of the house before she spoke. Her slice of pizza sat on her plate, forgotten. "You should have run the Blue Haven thing by me before you mentioned it to Lindsey."

"Don't you want to go?" He took a bite of pizza, pretending nonchalance.

"We can't go," Annie said. "We're only pretending to date because of Lindsey. People will talk when we don't act like normal couples act."

"Then we'll act like a normal couple."

She shook her head. "It's too risky, especially since they already know Lindsey is here visiting."

"They know a *family friend* is visiting," he said.

"What if someone gets suspicious?" Her fingers drummed on the tabletop.

"If we do the things normal couples do, like meeting friends for drinks, why would anybody get suspicious?"

"We could just say Lindsey can't babysit." Even though she was still trying to weasel out of the date, she spoke of them as a unit, which he took as a positive sign.

"You're forgetting something. *Lindsey* is the one we don't want to make suspicious." Ryan reached across the table and captured her hand, stilling her drumming fingers. Her eyes flew to his, her mouth parting.

The door banged open, admitting girl and dog. Annie's hand slipped out from under his, and he felt the loss of her warmth.

"Success!" Lindsey shouted. "Hobo did his business outside."

"He's training you as much as you're training him," Ryan remarked a moment before his cell phone rang.

"Is that the theme song from *ER?*" Lindsey asked.

"Of course not." He dug his phone out of his pocket as he answered. "Not all doctors watch medical dramas."

The phone played another line of the song.

"That's the *Scrubs* theme song!" Lindsey exclaimed. "You do too watch doctor shows."

He checked the number, confirming that the caller was Chase Bradford. "It's Chase. What should I tell him?"

"I'll do it," Lindsey said. "That way you two can go out."

Ryan slanted a questioning look at Annie, feeling as though he was asking her about more than whether she'd get together with his friends.

Her nod was almost imperceptible, but it was enough.

CHAPTER EIGHT

ANNIE SCOOTED sideways, barely getting out of the way of the shopping bag the woman coming toward her was swinging. Behind the woman the mall was filled with a mass of people, their shoes making clicking sounds on the polished surface of the tile floor, their faces oddly bright.

Annie grimaced, feeling a headache coming on. She hoped Lindsey was happy because she sure wasn't.

"This is great!" Lindsey exclaimed. "I can't believe you haven't been here before."

Lindsey obviously didn't know her very well. Annie wouldn't have agreed to drive more than an hour to the three-story mall in the far western suburbs of Philadelphia if she hadn't been trying to connect with Lindsey. The teenager had lobbied hard to come here after discovering the river rafters didn't run trips on Tuesdays, arranging to leave Hobo with a guide she'd befriended, then persuading Annie to close the shop at noon.

The girl was beaming as she checked out the window displays on either side of them, her long hair swinging from left to right. She was in her element; Annie wasn't. No matter how much Annie wished for it, there probably wouldn't be a whole lot of bonding going on.

"Okay. First priority is finding you something to wear on your date tonight," Lindsey said.

"Oh, no," Annie said. That wasn't part of the deal. "I have lots of clothes."

"Lots of *outdoorsy* clothes. Not lots of date clothes." Lindsey looked good enough to go out on a date herself. She wore a neutral-colored, sleeveless print baby doll dress she'd paired with wooden wedges that must be hell to walk in. "Don't you want to look pretty for Ryan?"

She shouldn't want to.

"That's not high on my list of priorities," Annie said.

"Why not?" Lindsey sounded alarmed. "I thought you liked him."

"I do like him," Annie immediately reassured her, then realized she'd spoken the truth.

"Then why not dress up for him?"

The short answer was that she intended to keep their relationship friendly instead of romantic. She couldn't tell Lindsey that so seized on the opportunity to impart some motherly wisdom.

"If a person can't see past your appearance to who you really are," Annie said, "he isn't worth your time."

"Is that why you still have that birthmark?"

Annie's step faltered. Nobody else asked her about the port-wine stain—ever—but this was the second time Lindsey had brought it up.

"I suppose so," Annie muttered.

"So it's a test to see if people like you for you?"

"I didn't say that."

"Don't get uptight," Lindsey said. "I'm trying to understand why you still have the thing. I mean, it obviously bothers you."

"It doesn't bother me," Annie denied.

"Then why are you always touching it?"

Annie felt the weight of her fingertips on her cheek and dropped her hand.

"There's a cosmetics store at this mall," Lindsey said. "We could get somebody to do your makeup. Places like that do an awesome job. They could cover it up for sure."

"I'm not going to a makeup store."

"But—"

"What kind of outfit do you think I should wear tonight?" Annie interrupted.

Lindsey stopped suddenly, pointing to a mannequin in a window display dressed in a slinky red sundress. "Something sexy. Like that!"

The birthmark apparently forgotten, Lindsey headed for the store as if an unseen force was propelling her forward. Moving impossibly fast in her wedge-soled shoes, she wove through the store like a pro until she located the sundresses. Annie had no choice but to follow.

Lindsey shuffled through the rack, pulling the red one out, guessing Annie's size right the first time. The garment looked even skimpier than it had on the model.

"I don't think that's going to work," Annie said, instead of ripping it from Lindsey's hand and putting it back on the rack the way she wanted to.

"That's why you need choices." Lindsey zigzagged through the displays, pulling dresses off the racks and handing them to Annie until her arms were overloaded.

"This is too many," Annie protested.

"The more dresses you try on, the better chance we have of finding the perfect one." Lindsey took half the dresses from her and folded them over her arm. "Come on. The dressing room's over here."

Figuring she didn't have a choice, Annie followed. She tried on a number of dresses that Lindsey rejected for various reasons until she got to the red one. The dressing-room mirror confirmed her initial impression. Her bruises from the bike accident had already faded, but the neckline plunged into a deep V, the material clung to her and it was way too short.

"You have the red one on, don't you?" Lindsey asked excitedly from outside the dressing room. "I can't wait to see it!"

Annie took a deep breath, then swung open the thin door.

Lindsey clapped her hands. "You look beautiful! That's the one. That's the dress."

"I'm not wearing this to the Blue Haven," Annie stated. The cut was too sexy, not to mention she'd heard that a recent study had concluded the color red made men feel more amorous toward women. "It's too…red."

"It's perfect," Lindsey protested. "You have to buy it."

"I'm not buying this dress," Annie said forcefully.

"Fine." Lindsey's features tightened. She reached into the dressing room, yanked out the garments Annie had already tried on and marched back through the store.

Annie battled despair as she returned to the dressing room and slipped out of the slinky dress. She'd planned to bond with Lindsey, not to snap at her.

She was in her underwear, taking another dress off a hanger when she heard footsteps, then a knock on the door. She opened it a crack, which immediately filled with something green. "Try this," Lindsey said.

It was the same dress in a different color. She sighed, expecting to find it no more suitable than the red one, then put it on. The dress fit her the same way, but the more subtle color changed everything. She turned this way and that, amazed at how good she looked.

"Well?" Lindsey asked loudly, sounding impatient.

This time Annie was smiling when she opened the door. "I love it."

"Me, too." The girl's gaze dropped to Annie's sturdy sandals. "But we have to do something about those shoes."

"THAT WAS a blast!" Lindsey said.

Other kids got a high from playing sports or music, but to Lindsey, nothing beat a day at the shopping center. A trip to a strip mall with her little brothers along didn't count.

The small back seat of the truck was full of stuff Lindsey had convinced Annie to buy, including a pair of strappy white sandals Annie could wear with the green dress.

Lindsey hadn't done so bad herself. She'd scored a really cute top and a paisley-print skirt. Lindsey would rather have had the tighter, shorter black skirt, but let Annie choose because she was buying.

She still wasn't happy about Annie telling Jason how old she was, but Annie wasn't so bad. Even when she was really busy, she made time for Lindsey.

"Now that I've gone shopping with you," Annie said, "you can come rafting with me."

"Oh, no!" Lindsey shook her head vehemently. "That is so not happening."

"Why not? I had fun shopping. What's to say you won't have a good time rafting?"

Was she serious? "You can shop on dry land."

"Getting wet isn't that big a deal."

"That's because you haven't seen my hair

when it loses body. It goes limp." Sunlight shone through the window, backlighting Annie's hair. "Yours does the same thing, doesn't it?"

"Not so much," Annie said, then backtracked. "Well, maybe a little, when it's humid."

"Then we'll use hot rollers tonight when I do your hair."

"I wasn't aware you were doing my hair," Annie said, "and I don't have hot rollers."

Who didn't have hot rollers? Annie sure needed her help bad. "My curling iron, then. After I get through with you, Ryan's gonna be drooling."

"Not if I chicken out and wear blue jeans."

"You can't!" Lindsey cried. "I know what you said before, but don't you want him to think you look hot?"

Annie didn't answer, but her cheeks reddened.

"You're blushing!" Lindsey exclaimed. "That's so romantic!"

"What's so romantic about a blush?"

"It means you really like him. So now you have to tell me how you met." Lindsey turned to face Annie so she had a better view of her, settling in for a story. She hoped it was sigh-worthy.

"I already told you," Annie said. "We met in high school."

"That's right." Lindsey thought of the book she was reading. The teenage characters had known they were destined to be together at first sight. "Were you into him back then, too?"

"We hardly knew each other." Annie looked at the highway instead of Lindsey. "We, uh, ran in different circles."

Lindsey figured that could only mean one thing. "He was popular and you weren't?"

"Something like that."

That made sense. Annie had probably been teased about her birthmark. The mark didn't bother Lindsey, but most high-school kids weren't as mature as she was.

"Ryan's still pretty cool," Lindsey said. "How did you get him to ask you out anyway?"

"I didn't *get* him to ask me out. We hadn't seen each other in a long time when I took you to the pediatrician's office," Annie said. "I guess he wanted to catch up."

"You mean I had something to do with you getting together?"

"You could say that," Annie said slowly.

"Sweet," Lindsey said.

She leaned back against her seat, thinking about how cool that was. Annie was letting her visit, and she was helping Annie with Ryan.

Making sure Annie looked great tonight, though, was just a start. It wouldn't kill Lindsey to do her part to get Ryan to keep coming around. That meant sacrifice.

"I'll come rafting on one condition," she said. "Ryan has to come, too."

CHAPTER NINE

TOBY BRADFORD had egg on his face.

The scrambled yellow stuff was also on his hands, smeared over his clothes and dotting his baby-fine blond hair.

So far Ryan was the only one in the Bradford kitchen who'd noticed the egg-splattered one-year-old. Annie had excused herself to use the restroom shortly after they'd delivered Lindsey for Tuesday-night babysitting detail. Kelly and Chase had their backs to the high chair as they gave Lindsey instructions. Lindsey probably couldn't see anything other than a talking wall of overprotectiveness.

Toby grinned at Ryan with an open mouth that showed gaps in his baby teeth. He lifted both chubby hands and patted the eggs stuck to them, pure joy crossing his face. It felt to Ryan as though he and the little boy were sharing a private joke. Toby picked up another handful of egg and the moment was over.

"Somebody better check on Toby," Ryan said, interrupting Kelly's recitation of the little boy's bedtime routine.

Both Kelly and Chase whirled just as the eggs flew. They didn't travel far, falling harmlessly to the kitchen floor.

"Toby!" Kelly was instantly at his side, whisking away the plate of scrambled eggs she'd given him for dinner. "Stop that!"

Toby's face fell at the loss of his entertainment. He seemed to shoot an accusatory look at Ryan.

"Sorry, bud," Ryan mouthed silently to the little boy.

"I'll get a washcloth," Chase told Kelly, springing into action but hiding a grin.

Kelly lifted Toby out of the high chair, holding him at arm's length. She was everything Chase had said she was: pretty, sweet and wild about the little boy Chase had discovered wasn't related by blood to either of them. An ex-girlfriend of Chase's who was serving a prison sentence had signed over custody of Toby, which was ironic considering the woman had tried to blame her crime on Kelly. The way Chase told it, he'd met Kelly while she was trying to exonerate herself. So Toby's birth mother was inadvertently responsible for getting them together.

"What were you trying to do?" Kelly asked Toby, her voice indulgent. "Scare away the babysitter?"

"It'd take more than that to scare me," Lindsey said. "I have two little brothers."

"Then you know how handy paper towels are," Kelly said. "Can you get me some? They're beside the sink."

Lindsey located them, pulling off a few. Ryan went to help her, turning on the faucet so she could wet them.

"Girls are just as messy," Ryan said as they worked.

Lindsey reached the high chair at the same time Chase reentered the kitchen with a washcloth and a towel. She wiped up the tray while Chase helped Kelly strip off the baby's clothes and clean him up. Ryan grabbed some fresh paper towels from the roll, exchanging them for the ones Lindsey had soiled.

"I was never messy," Lindsey proclaimed.

Ryan had no way of knowing if that were true. Lindsey was his daughter, but he'd never seen her as a baby.

He dumped the used paper towels in the trash can beneath the sink, his mind whirring.

This wasn't the first time he'd thought about Lindsey's childhood.

Even before he'd learned his daughter's name and what had become of her, he'd wondered about her. Every time his work had brought him in touch with babies, he'd thought of her. The first time Ryan had delivered a baby, he could hardly see through the tears. He'd missed his own child's arrival.

"Lindsey, give those paper towels to Chase so he can wipe up the floor. I need you to hold Toby while I get him some clean clothes." Kelly even had a sweetness about her when she gave orders.

Annie walked into the kitchen, stepping gingerly on high heels he guessed she wasn't used to walking in. He'd always liked the way she looked, but her green dress emphasized how truly lovely she was. No, not lovely. That was too mild a word. Stunning. He'd barely been able to speak when he first saw her. In the car, he'd had trouble keeping his eyes off her and on the road.

She was just in time to see Lindsey take the baby, who was now clad only in a diaper. Toby snuggled against the teenager, leaning his blond head against her chest. Lindsey picked bits of egg from his hair.

Ryan stared at the two of them, his throat going dry. He exchanged a glance with Annie, who appeared as staggered as he felt. All the moments of Lindsey's life they hadn't been part of came into sharper focus. They hadn't walked her to the bus stop for school, slipped money under her pillow when she'd lost her first tooth or wiped her nose when she was sick.

Ryan hadn't done anything but give Lindsey up without a fight or even much thought. He'd let Annie go with hardly any protest, too, although he'd never connected with anyone on a deeper level than he had with her during that amazing night they'd shared.

If he'd possessed the strength of character to suggest they keep their baby, he might not be here in Chase Bradford's kitchen regretting what might have been.

Had Annie agreed, she wouldn't have been a stranger for the past fourteen years. He didn't delude himself that the road would have been easy. They'd been too young to marry and possibly too immature to stay together through the demands of raising a child.

Loving their daughter, however, might have led them to love each other.

Kelly returned to the kitchen with a change

of clothes, and Lindsey laughed at Chase's crack about Toby making a bigger mess than Humpty Dumpty. Her young face hinted at what she might have looked like at Toby's age.

"Looks like I missed something," Annie said.

"We both did," Ryan said softly. "We missed a lot."

ANNIE HAD probably been inside the Blue Haven Pub on a hundred different occasions, but this time she hesitated outside the door.

Ryan's warm hand instantly rested against the small of her back, his voice soft in her ear. "Don't be nervous. Think of it as meeting friends for drinks."

It was the first thing he'd said since they'd left the Bradford house. During the ride to the bar, he'd been subdued. Thinking about missing out on Lindsey's childhood, she supposed. She thought about it, too. A lot. She didn't, however, wish to discuss it.

"Friends who think we're involved," she said.

"Kelly and Chase didn't have any trouble believing that."

They'd originally planned to ride to the bar with the other couple, but Kelly and Chase were still dealing with the aftermath of the egg incident. Kelly had urged them to go ahead so all four of them wouldn't be late.

"Kelly and Chase were distracted," Annie said.

"You're distracting me in that dress," he said.

This wasn't the first time tonight he'd commented on her appearance, although Lindsey had practically insisted he give his reaction to the dress. He hadn't disappointed the girl, lavishing Annie with compliments.

"You don't have to say things like that when nobody else can hear," Annie said.

"What if you look so beautiful I can't help myself?" His breath tickled her ear.

Annie knew she looked good. The dress flattered her, and Lindsey had curled her hair to make it fall in soft waves around her bare shoulders. The girl had done her makeup, too, although Annie had stopped her when she tried to cover the port-wine stain.

But beautiful? She hardly thought so.

His hand exerted gentle pressure at her back, propelling her forward. She wouldn't take his comments too seriously. She could handle a friendship with him but nothing more.

Look at how she'd reacted to his kiss at the miniature golf course.

She reminded herself she'd goaded him

into the kiss and shoved it out of her mind, the same way she had since it had happened. It hadn't been real, just as tonight wasn't real.

"Over here!" Johnny Pollock waved them over to a table at the back of the bar. His wife Penelope's chair was flush against his so there wasn't any space between them. Michael Donahue had his arm around Sara Brenneman.

Annie was so hyperaware of being watched she might have stopped walking if not for Ryan's gentle prodding. She touched her cheek, then remembered what Lindsey had said and dropped her hand. "I don't think we can pull this off," she murmured under her breath.

Ryan placed his hand on her waist, holding her so close his intoxicating scent overrode the faint bar smell of beer and the peanuts the staff put out on every table. "Sure we can."

After they reached their group and explained that Chase and Kelly were running late, Johnny made sure everybody was acquainted. Annie had gone to high school with Michael and Johnny and had met Sara several times. Sara looked stunning in red pants and a sleeveless top shot through with jagged red-and-black lines. Annie knew Johnny's wife, Penelope, less well.

"Annie runs Indigo River Rafters," Johnny repeated the increasingly common misconception to his wife.

"Only until my dad gets back from Poland." Annie hadn't spoken to her father since he'd phoned the morning after she'd found out about Lindsey and told her what he knew about the girl's life. Until she was ready to forgive him, she couldn't bring herself to keep in regular contact. "I'm still with the magazine."

"What magazine?" Penelope asked.

"Annie's a staff writer for *Outdoor Women*," Ryan said. "Impressive, isn't it?"

"I'll say," Penelope rejoined, then asked so many questions about working for a magazine that Annie was relieved when the arrival of Kelly and Chase took the spotlight off her.

"There was so much egg in Toby's hair we gave him a bath," Kelly explained. "I didn't want Lindsey to have to do it alone the first time she babysat."

"Who's Lindsey?" Penelope asked.

Annie's muscles knotted as they did every time somebody asked about the girl. Ryan's hand covered hers, giving it a reassuring squeeze.

"She's a friend of Annie's family," he answered easily. "She's in town for a visit."

Annie prepared herself to be bombarded with personal questions about Lindsey, mentally readying the careful responses she'd devised.

"She helped pick out Annie's dress," Kelly said.

"I've been meaning to tell you it looks great," Sara said. "That style is perfect on you."

Annie let herself relax a little. "Thanks."

"Lindsey told me you got it at the mall," Kelly interjected.

"Not my favorite place," Annie said, "but I did get Lindsey to agree to go rafting with me and Ryan in exchange."

"Oh, really?" Ryan asked.

"I didn't get around to telling you yet," Annie said, "but saying you'd go was the only way she'd agree."

"Then I'm there."

Ryan kept hold of her hand, a good idea. It gave the impression they were really together. His thumb caressed the inside of her wrist, an unnecessary touch. A shiver ran through her.

"If Lindsey wants to go shopping again, I'll take her," Sara said. "Look how great Annie looks tonight."

"You're giving Lindsey too much credit."

Ryan picked up their linked hands, lacing his fingers through hers. "Annie looks fantastic in whatever she wears."

He was pouring it on too thick. Annie's pulse raced. Her cheeks, she felt certain, had reddened. Surely everybody else at the table had noticed he was trying too hard.

"I agree with that," Johnny said, "but be careful of my buddy there, Annie. He's always been a smooth operator."

"I've never been a smooth operator," Ryan protested. "Why do you think I didn't become a surgeon?"

Everybody laughed, although Annie had to force hers. Johnny was right. She couldn't start believing Ryan meant what he said, especially since their goal tonight was to be convincing as a couple. Even if it weren't, she knew better than to fall for Ryan a second time.

The conversation drifted to other topics. Through a backdrop of jukebox music and a TV baseball game that was turned up too loud, Annie found out Ryan had gone to med school at Temple University and did his residency at a hospital in Philadelphia.

"How were you able to drop everything to help out your sister?" Chase asked.

"There was nothing to drop," Ryan said.

"After my residency, I filled in for a doctor on maternity leave at a health center in the city. She came back right when Sierra broke her leg."

Annie had assumed Ryan had taken a high-paying position after his residency ended, although she couldn't say for certain where she'd gotten that impression. Maybe from the Lexus, except she'd discovered tonight the car belonged to his sister. His own car was a hybrid.

"Weren't you at the health center Sunday?" Michael asked Ryan. "Isn't that why you couldn't play pickup basketball?"

Ryan shifted as though he wasn't comfortable answering. "Yeah. They needed someone to help out."

So that's where Ryan had been on Sunday before he found Hobo. Annie's opinion of him slowly shifted from a flashy young doctor out to make a buck to a man who was socially and environmentally conscious.

"Will you stay on at your sister's practice after her leg heals?" Sara asked, her head resting against Michael's shoulder.

"I haven't decided," Ryan said. "I have some feelers out for jobs, but I could go in a couple of directions. That's one of them."

Another stunner. How could Annie have been unaware that Ryan was considering living in Indigo Springs permanently? Although she spent most of her time on the road, she did make regular visits home. If Ryan were a town resident, it would be difficult to avoid him in the future.

She looked down at their hands, which had been entwined for most of the evening. Who was she kidding? The more time she spent with Ryan, the less able she'd be to keep her distance. No matter where he chose to live, they couldn't go back to being strangers.

She thought she could handle letting him into her life—as long as she could keep him out of her heart.

RYAN WONDERED as the evening at the Blue Haven wore on what it said about him that he was perfectly willing to take advantage of the situation.

He enjoyed holding Annie's hand without having her yank it away. He liked that she couldn't question every nice thing he said to her. He was keen on his friends thinking of them as a couple.

The growing attraction he felt for Annie could be due to Lindsey. When he'd realized earlier that evening how much of Lindsey's childhood he'd missed, it had forcefully brought home to him that he and Annie had produced a living, breathing miracle.

But he didn't think that was all of it.

Even without Lindsey around, he got pure pleasure from being with Annie.

Penelope leaned forward, interest blooming on her face. "How long have the two of you been dating?"

Ryan put his arm around Annie, drawing her close, enjoying the sharp intake of breath nobody else could hear. "Since last week."

"Tell me," Penelope said, putting her elbows on the table and looking from one of them to the other, "what made you two hook up?"

Ryan felt Annie's muscles seize.

"You know, you don't have to answer all of my wife's questions," Johnny said.

"Penelope fancies herself a matchmaker." Sara patted her friend's arm. "She's constantly trying to figure out who should be dating who and why."

"What's wrong with that?" Penelope asked.

"I'll tell you what," Johnny said, but he was smiling. "You're constantly asking people questions that are none of your business."

"I am not!" Penelope straightened and picked up her glass of white wine but didn't drink from it. "So, Ryan, didn't I hear somewhere that you were coming off a really bad relationship? This isn't a rebound thing, is it?"

"Penelope!" Johnny chastised. "Ryan, ignore her."

"I don't mind answering," Ryan said. It would enable him to let Annie know he wasn't the smooth operator Johnny had alluded to earlier that evening. "You have me confused with someone else. When you're in med school and doing a residency, you barely have time to sleep, let alone be in a relationship."

"Maybe it was that new vet who had the serious girlfriend," Penelope said almost to herself, before switching her attention to Annie. "How about you, Annie?"

"Nope," Annie said. "No serious girlfriends."

Everybody laughed, even Ryan, although he'd have liked to hear the answer. Annie was so closemouthed about herself he knew nothing about her dating history.

He excused himself to go to the restroom. On the way back, he heard someone call his name. Jim Waverly, a former high-school classmate he'd never much liked, was sitting at the bar.

Ryan plastered on a smile and shook the other man's hand. "How's it going?"

"Better now since I'm divorced," Waverly

said. Ryan hadn't run into the man since returning to Indigo Springs, but remembered somebody saying his wife had caught him cheating. "I like being a free agent. How 'bout you?"

"Never been married."

"Yeah, I heard that." He nodded toward Ryan's friends. "Strange to see you over there with Sublinski. Wouldn't have known it was her if not for that thing on her face. You'd have thought she'd gotten rid of it by now."

"I think she looks great." Ryan backed away from the other man, loathe to associate with him. "I need to get back to my friends."

On his way back to the table, he was surprised to see Chad Armstrong sitting at a booth with a stuffy-looking couple he didn't recognize. Ryan hadn't checked with Sierra about her plans but she must have passed up an evening at the Blue Haven. He exchanged a silent nod with Chad.

The time passed quickly after that. When eleven o'clock rolled around, Michael called it a night.

"Sara's been using my shoulder as a pillow for the past hour," he said. "I've got to get her home to bed."

"Okay," she told him, eyes twinkling. He laughed and kissed her briefly on the lips.

Soon all eight of them walked into the night, with Ryan and Annie heading in the same direction as the Pollocks.

"I'm sorry if I was too nosy," Penelope said. "It's just that I never would have put you two together, but now I'm convinced you're perfect for each other."

Ryan wasn't about to argue with that.

He didn't comment on Penelope's observation until he and Annie were inside his car, driving through the quiet town en route to pick up Lindsey.

"So the town matchmaker thinks we're perfect for each other. What do you make of that?"

"What does Jim Waverly think?" she asked. "I saw you talking to him."

The change of subject threw him. "I don't care what he thinks."

"You didn't mention Lindsey, did you? You didn't say she was in town?"

Those were strange questions. "Why would I?"

She shifted in her seat. "I guess because you two used to be friends."

"Not really." Waverly had been buddies

with some of Ryan's friends, which was another thing entirely. His memory was hazy, but he thought Waverly might have been the one who'd made a pass at Annie the night he'd driven her home from the party. No use bringing that up, though.

He left the main road for the residential neighborhood where Chase lived with Kelly and Toby. The other couple's car was already in the driveway.

Lindsey must have been watching for them because she skipped out of the house, waving goodbye to Kelly. She got into the back seat, full of stories about Toby.

"Don't you want to know if we had a good time?" Ryan asked when she finally paused for breath.

"Oh, yeah." Lindsey's voice was young and eager. "How'd it go?"

"It went great." Ryan slanted Annie a look. "Annie looked so beautiful I couldn't take my eyes off her."

"I told you that dress was perfect!" Lindsey exclaimed, then went back to her rendition of the night, sounding as comfortable as if she'd grown up with them as her parents.

It felt, Ryan thought, as though the three

of them were a real family. Just like tonight
Annie had seemed to be his real girlfriend.

That was what he wanted, he realized. He
just needed to figure out how to make it happen.

CHAPTER TEN

A THICK STREAM of water arced through the warm summer air, its destination the back of Lindsey's head. Annie didn't even have time to shout a warning.

The water hit its mark, cascading over Lindsey in a cool shower. She shouted in shock, her hands lifting futilely to cover her already drenched hair.

The family of four in the next raft roared with laughter, the loudest hoots coming from the teenage boy of about sixteen who held the white plastic container.

"Why did he do that?" Lindsey asked indignantly.

She did indignation well, so well she'd almost weaseled out of the deal to go rafting. Annie would have let her, even though she'd arranged for two other guides to come so she didn't have to work the trip. Ryan wouldn't hear of it, not after he'd already taken Wednesday afternoon off.

"Water fights break out between rapids when it's hot," Annie said, hearing the apology in her voice. "It's kind of a tradition."

"It stinks!" Lindsey cried. She pushed her wet hair back from her face, which wouldn't have been necessary if she'd worn it in a ponytail as Annie had suggested.

"Only if you don't fight back," Ryan said. Each raft had a container, its intended purpose to bail out the water that inevitably collected at the bottom of the raft. Ryan tried to hand Lindsey theirs. "Here."

She settled her hands on her hips, looking like bedraggled royalty. "You can't be serious."

"They're probably over there planning another attack," Ryan said. "You want them to pick on you for the rest of the trip?"

Her expression turning fierce, Lindsey grabbed the pail from him and dipped it into the river. With the muscles in her upper arms straining, she swung the bucket backward, then put all her weight into a forward motion. The water hit the teenage boy square in the chest.

"She's a ringer!" Ryan shouted. Lindsey beamed, and she and Ryan exchanged a high five.

He'd handled the situation perfectly, Annie thought, much better than she would have if she and Lindsey had been alone. He'd make a terrific dad, yet another point in his favor. Annie gave herself a mental shake. That kind of thinking was dangerous.

"You've done it now," the teenage boy yelled. He refilled his container and let the water fly. Lindsey ducked, putting her head in her lap and covering up. The stream caught Ryan. He gasped, reacting to the cool shock of the water.

Lifting her head, Lindsey giggled. Lines appeared at the corners of Ryan's eyes, crinkling in amusement. His smile flashed.

"Get the other bucket, Annie!" he yelled, pointing behind her to where a second container sat. "We'll teach them to mess with us."

He handed Lindsey the first pail and encouraged Annie to load the second. Under Ryan's direction, the two of them launched a double-pronged attack. They managed to hit all four people in the other raft with two tosses of water.

Ryan raised a fist in the air. "Those are my girls!"

The water fight didn't stop there. By the end of the battle, everybody in the two rafts was soaked and laughing. Lindsey's makeup had washed off so she looked about, well, thirteen years old.

Most of her ferocity disappeared when they tackled the rapids. This was a pleasure trip, with the course no more than medium difficult even in the most challenging of times. Summer rafting tended to be tame, especially when rainfall was low, as it had been for the past few weeks. Lindsey still screamed her way through the rapids, her cries louder than the roar of the white water.

The rest of the afternoon passed in much the same vein, with the teenager in the other raft resuming the water fight between rapids. He called a truce when they stopped for lunch, inviting Lindsey over to the shady spot he and his younger brother had picked to eat their sandwiches.

Ryan claimed the space next to Annie, sitting on a wide, flat rock that afforded a spectacular view of the winding river. With the sun shining, the water shimmered, the sky seemed more blue and the bushes and trees along the riverside took on deeper shades of green. Ryan was more interested in the sight of Lindsey and her new friends. Lindsey ate with gusto instead of picking at her food as she sometimes did. Between bites, she laughed at whatever the boys were telling her.

"She's having fun, don't you think?" Annie asked Ryan.

"Oh, yeah, but she might not admit it," Ryan said. "She doesn't think of herself as an outdoor woman."

She smiled at his reference to her magazine. "I can live with that as long as she's enjoying herself."

"I'm enjoying myself, too," he said. "That's not hard to do with you around."

"There you go again saying nice things when no one else is around," she said as lightly as she could, watching Lindsey instead of him. The girl and the two brothers sat with their feet dangling in the water, alternately kicking up spray.

"I ran into Johnny this morning. He had some nice things to say about you, too," Ryan said. "Everybody had such a good time Tuesday they're planning to meet monthly. We're invited."

Since she wasn't looking at him, she had a better chance of hiding her wistfulness that things could be different. "I'm sure you can come up with some excuse next month about why we can't join them."

"I know you're not dating anyone else right now, but is there somebody you care about?" he asked. "You were pretty evasive when Penelope asked."

"That's not it." She figured it wouldn't hurt to tell him about her last relationship. "It's been about three years since I had a serious boyfriend."

"What happened?"

"He wanted to get married. I didn't." She left it at that, although the sticking point had been more complicated. To her ex, marriage included children. By giving up Lindsey, she'd already proven that she was no more cut out for that kind of a life than the mother who'd abandoned her when she was a child. Especially with a man she didn't love.

"Then why can't we join them?" Ryan asked. "Your dad won't be back for another month. You'll still be in town."

"Lindsey will be gone." She turned to face him, determined to make her position clear. "Once she leaves, we can stop pretending."

"I'm not pretending."

She'd half expected him to say something like that, which was why she'd tried so hard since last night not to be alone with him.

"I'm attracted to you, Annie." A lock of her

hair had fallen in her eyes. He smoothed it back from her face, his fingertips brushing her cheek. She told herself she didn't shy away from his touch because Lindsey could be watching. "So why don't we keep dating and see where it goes?"

She shook her head back and forth vehemently. "No."

"Why not?" he said. "I think you're attracted to me, too."

She ignored his remark, unwilling to admit it was true. "The only reason we're together is Lindsey and she's going home soon."

"Maybe she'll come back."

"What? Where is this coming from?"

"Look at her, Annie," he said. Lindsey was knee-deep in river water, her hair falling in her face. She splashed the younger of the two brothers, her laughter traveling on the breeze when he retaliated. "Does that look like the sullen, unhappy girl her stepmother talked about? She's thriving here. She's even eating more. Why shouldn't she come back to visit?"

Annie saw the same things in Lindsey he did, but she couldn't let herself be blinded by them. One of them had to be realistic. "It's a fluke that she's here now, Ryan. She didn't come to visit us, so why would her parents let her come back?"

"*We're* her parents."

"The people who *raised* her are her parents," she corrected. "We gave her up, and that's what we're going to have to do again. Soon."

He picked up a small rock and flung it into the river, away from where the rafters were eating their lunches. "It doesn't have to be like that. We can keep in touch with her."

"What reason would we give?" she asked, although he hadn't brought up anything she hadn't thought of herself, anything she hadn't daydreamed about. "Do you really think it would be fair to complicate her life like that?'

He didn't respond. The closed look on his face told her she hadn't gotten through to him.

"I'm not ready to give up on her," he said. "I'm not ready to give up on *you*."

"You'll have to. Once Lindsey is gone, things between us will be over." She stood up before he had a chance to respond, not wanting to hear any more from him. She clapped her hands, then announced to the group. "Gather up your trash. It's time to go."

She could no more trust the feelings Ryan professed to have for her than the fantasy that

Lindsey could continue to be part of their lives.

She'd stopped believing in fairy tales a long time ago.

ANNIE WAS DOING her best to put distance between them, and so far Ryan hadn't been able to do anything about it.

The cold shoulder had started after lunch when they'd gotten back in the raft for the second half of the trip. She was the most experienced rafter by far, but she'd let him do the heavy paddling, sitting in the front with Lindsey rather than in back with him. Even Lindsey had noticed the imbalance, moving to the rear of the raft to even things out.

The chill had continued once they reached land, with Annie hanging behind to supervise the crew that was taking the rafts from the river. She'd advised Lindsey and Ryan to go ahead to the shop.

Lindsey hadn't needed to be told twice, rushing ahead so she could reunite with Hobo.

"How's the voice?" Ryan asked her.

"Fine." Lindsey was kneeling beside Hobo, who was smothering her with love as though he hadn't seen her in years instead of hours. "Why would anything be wrong with my voice?"

"You sure screamed enough," he teased.

"That's because people kept throwing water at me," she complained loudly. The teenage boy who'd instigated the water fight was moving away from the checkout counter, a can of soda in hand.

He was a tall, handsome boy who swaggered when he walked. He grinned at her. "Only because you look cute when you're wet."

Ryan nearly told the boy how old Lindsey was, then Lindsey stuck her tongue out at him, showing her age. The boy laughed, lifting a hand in farewell as he walked to the exit.

"My son's a good kid, but he can be a little obnoxious." The adult man who'd been in the raft with the two boys was still in the shop, probably to pick up his keys, which rafters could leave behind the counter for safekeeping so they didn't have to worry about losing them in the river.

"It was all in good fun," Ryan said. "No need to apologize."

"That wasn't an apology." The man had the same tall, strong build as his son. "Our raft got slammed. Your family gave back as good as it got."

Lindsey glanced up sharply from petting Hobo. "Ryan and Annie aren't my parents."

The man's brows drew together, his gaze moving between them, his mouth slightly agape. "I'm sorry. I just assumed he was your dad."

Lindsey went back to petting Hobo, muttering something under her breath that sounded like, "I wish."

At her comment, a dozen scenarios ran through Ryan's head, a hundred questions buzzed in his brain about Lindsey's situation at home. After the other man left the shop, Ryan was plotting how to get Lindsey alone to talk when Hobo barked.

"Good dog!" Lindsey said. She fastened the leash on his collar, remarking to Ryan, "He's telling me he needs to go outside. Isn't that great?"

He followed her out past the picnic tables, glad he'd bought a leash with a fifteen-foot retractable cord. He didn't want any distractions, not even from Hobo.

He couldn't think of a way to casually bring up the subject so came out with it. "What's your dad like?"

She'd changed out of her waterproof sandals into tennis shoes. She scuffed one of them in the grass. "He's okay, I guess."

"Okay? I thought you two were close."

She made a face. "Where'd you get that idea?"

Why had he assumed Lindsey and her adoptive father were close? He supposed from the bits and pieces Annie had told him about Lindsey's life. She'd said there was friction between Lindsey and her stepmother, and he'd automatically assumed she had a better relationship with her father.

"Don't you get along with him?" he asked.

"More or less." She scraped her feet some more. "When I see him."

"Does he work a lot?"

"Not so much." She lifted her head, her eyes on Hobo, who had found a convenient tree to shower. "He's a manager at the post office. He goes in early so he can come home early."

"Then why don't you see him more?" It felt like he was pulling the answers from her.

"I used to," she said, "but now Timmy and Teddy are old enough that they play some stupid sport or other all year long. My dad's always with them."

"You don't play a sport?"

She snorted. "I hate sports."

"Then what do you do for fun?" he asked. "Besides shop and sleep, that is."

She didn't react to his teasing. Neither did

she pay attention to Hobo, who was running in circles, apparently chasing his tail. "I want to get into modeling. One of the girls at school is in those glossy store ads that come with the newspaper. I want to do that."

Modeling wasn't as much of a pipe dream as it seemed. Ryan had seen it work out for somebody who used to look a lot like Lindsey. "My sister did some modeling when she was a teenager."

"Really?" Her voice spiked with interest. "What kind?"

"Print ads mostly," he said. "My mom sent her photos to some talent agencies in Philadelphia. The one that signed her got her a few jobs. Mom used to take her into the city for photo shoots, usually on weekends."

"Do you think she'd talk to me about it, maybe give me some tips?" Lindsey asked, completely focused on the subject. Behind her, Hobo had stopped going around and around. He wasn't traveling in a straight line, either. He was weaving as if he was dizzy.

Ryan hesitated before answering. It would be awkward for Sierra and Lindsey to get together with neither of them realizing there was something similar about them. "It's still tough for Sierra to get around with that broken leg. You might not like what she has to say, either. She got tired of modeling pretty fast."

"I'd never get tired of it," Lindsey said dramatically. "But that doesn't matter to my dad."

"He doesn't want you to try it?"

"He doesn't care what I do," she said bitterly. It was a cloudless day with the sun illuminating every nuance in her dejected expression. "He just doesn't want to miss any of my brothers' stupid games."

"Did he tell you that?"

"He didn't have to. A couple of weeks ago I asked that girl at school who her photographer was. I finally got my dad to let me make an appointment. At the last minute he couldn't drive me because he had stuff to do. Do you know what that stuff was? He took my little brothers fishing!"

"How about your stepmother? Couldn't she have taken you?"

"She's busy all the time. Cooking and cleaning and working."

"Do you get along with her?"

"She's not so bad." A sad expression crossed Lindsey's face. "But she's not really my mother. She's Timmy and Teddy's mother. My mother's dead."

Except that wasn't precisely true. Lindsey's

adoptive mother, to whom he and Annie owed a world of gratitude, was dead. Lindsey's birth mother was very much alive. Her birth father was, too.

Hobo, apparently recovered from his dizzying antics, bounded toward them. Lindsey bent down to pet him.

"Have you asked your dad to spend more time with you?" Ryan asked.

"It wouldn't do any good," she said, burying her face in the dog's fur. "He's not the one who wanted me."

"Who told you that?"

"My grandpa. He's my mom's dad. He said she wanted a baby worse than anything and that she loved me more than life. It didn't matter to her that I was adopted."

"That doesn't mean your dad didn't want you, too."

"Not in the same way he wanted my brothers. He's always saying how much they look like him when he was a kid. They're even all left-handed." She sniffed. "I know he loves them more than me."

Ryan cast around for something reassuring to say. "Your dad doesn't love your brothers more than you because they're all lefties."

Lindsey stood up. She hadn't touched up

her makeup and her hair was messier than he'd ever seen it, but the childish quality that had hung over her all afternoon had vanished.

"I know that," she said. "He loves them more because they're really his."

QUIET FILLED the house, which happened every night when Lindsey retreated to her bedroom and shut the door. She took Hobo with her, having convinced Annie that the dog was better off sleeping at the foot of her bed than beside the sofa. Annie suspected Hobo sneaked into bed with her, but didn't make an issue of it.

Annie usually straightened the house, then settled down with a book until her eyelids got too heavy to read and she went to sleep. Tonight she did neither because of the man in her living room leafing through a copy of *Outdoor Women*.

Ryan looked up at her when she entered the great room. "You're an excellent writer. I'm reading your story about backpacking through Glacier National Park. I've never been to Montana, but I can see those vast stretches of green pasture and that big blue sky."

Annie didn't let his praise sidetrack her because she suspected that was his intent.

She'd dropped a half-dozen broad hints for him to leave since the rafting trip had ended. "Why are you still here, Ryan?"

He closed the magazine and set it on the coffee table. "I needed to talk to you alone."

"We already talked at the river."

"Not about what Lindsey told me this afternoon about her family," he said in a soft voice.

The girl hadn't confided in Annie except to make passing comments suggesting she wasn't happy at home. Annie had lost sleep at night trying to figure out how to get her to open up, yet Ryan seemed to have done it effortlessly. She wanted to hear what Ryan had discovered more than she wanted him to leave.

"Come on," she told him. "We can't talk here."

Although it probably would have been safe to talk on the porch, Annie wasn't willing to take the chance. She descended the porch steps and walked with Ryan over the expanse of lawn between the house and the business.

The trees near the river didn't grow as thickly, letting in the glow from the moon. Day had turned into night, bringing clouds that obscured most of the light so they couldn't make out the river.

The collection of tables outside the shop

was mostly in shadows. She chose the farthest one and sat down, her knees facing outward. Ryan remained standing, the moon's faint light silhouetting him so he looked almost ethereal.

"Lindsey's problem isn't with her stepmother," Ryan said. "It's with her father. He wasn't the one who wanted to adopt her."

Annie's mind rebelled, even though the information jibed with what her father had told her over the phone about Helene Nowak Thompson pushing for the adoption. "How could you possibly know that?"

She listened with growing distress while Ryan repeated what Lindsey had shared, then desperately searched for a reason to explain the girl's perception that she wasn't wanted. "Her brothers are young. They need more attention than she does."

"If Lindsey was unhappy enough to run away from home," he reasoned, "there has to be something to what she says."

Annie hadn't called Lindsey's visit to Indigo Springs "running away." Surely that was an exaggeration. "Her stepmother said she'd never done anything like this before. If she's been so unhappy, why wait until now?"

He rubbed the back of his neck. "I think

not taking her to the photographer was the final straw."

Annie shook her head. She didn't want to hear this. The mental picture of Lindsey as a happy, well-adjusted child with an ideal home life had comforted her over the years.

"I think we should approach her adoptive father about letting her come to Indigo Springs for regular visits," Ryan stated.

The river water was gurgling, the cicadas were singing, the wind was rustling the leaves in the trees and an owl was hooting. She wanted to believe she hadn't heard him correctly, but none of the ambient noise had gotten in the way.

She shook her head, refusing to consider his suggestion. "That's crazy! Lindsey doesn't even know who we are!"

"Then we'll go to Pittsburgh to talk to Ted Thompson and his wife. We'll explain why we gave Lindsey up and make a case that we should be part of her life." He continued talking even though she was shaking her head back and forth. "We'll make them understand how much we love her."

"That won't fly," she said. "We don't have any legal claim on her."

"If it's what Lindsey wants, we might not

have to," Ryan said. "She's thirteen. She's old enough to have a say in this."

Annie put her hands to her head. She felt as if she was on a merry-go-round that wouldn't stop, her thoughts swirling. The notion she kept returning to over and over was that maybe it could work. Maybe they could keep Lindsey not only in their hearts, but in their lives.

Before hope took hold and blotted out reason, she tried to think, grasping for the hole in his argument. The carousel crashed to a stop when she found it because the flaw in his plan was as big as a crater.

"Lindsey's family life might not be perfect but it's stable. She has a father and a step-mother and brothers. Add us and it's like saddling her with a set of divorced parents."

"Not if we're together," he said.

The moon peeked out from behind a cloud, illuminating his face. She'd never seen him look more serious.

"I'm not saying this only because it would help our case with Lindsey." He moved a step toward her. She sat very still. "I meant what I said on the river today. I want to give what's between us a shot."

"There's nothing between us," she denied,

jumping to her feet, intending to return to the house. Instead of backing away, he took a step forward, trapping her between the picnic table and his body.

"You know that's not true." He laid a hand against her cheek. "You can feel it, the same way I do. There's always been something there."

The pain she'd suffered as a sixteen-year-old bubbled to the surface, nearly choking her. She knocked his hand away.

"No," she said. "It wouldn't work."

"It's already working," he argued, his eyes steady on hers. "Haven't you noticed what a good time we have together? Lindsey doesn't even have to be around. She wasn't there at the Blue Haven."

"No," she said again, more emphatically.

"I keep hearing the word but not a reason you're saying it." He sounded exasperated, frustration tugging at his features. "Why? Tell me one good reason you won't give us a shot?"

"Because I could never trust you."

He ran a hand over his lower face. "I'm not a kid anymore, Annie. I'd protect you. I'd never screw up like that again."

He'd misunderstood her, but that wasn't surprising. They'd never talked about his betrayal. It was possible, even likely, that he thought he'd pulled one over on her. She hadn't intended to discuss this with him, but it was the only way she could make him understand. She took a deep breath.

"I know about the bet, Ryan."

He blinked, confusion crossing his face. Was it possible it had been so long ago that he'd forgotten? That thought was almost as mortifying as the revelation had been.

"I know you and your friends challenged each other to see who could be the first to sleep with the girl with the birthmark." She willed her voice not to crack, for her hand not to cover her port-wine stain. "I know you won."

"No!" he denied. "That's not true."

"But you did sleep with me. You won the bet."

"You've got it wrong. Look, I knew about the bet. But I wasn't part of it."

How gullible did he think she was? Her stomach heaved and she felt as though she might be sick. "You just happened to see me leaving that party by myself and offered me a ride home? That was just a coincidence?"

"No," he admitted. "I followed you because—"

"You saw your buddy Jim Waverly hitting

on me." She finished the sentence for him, forcing herself to get everything in the open. "You were afraid he'd win."

Understanding dawned on his face. "That's why you asked about Waverly when we left the Blue Haven."

"Can you blame me?" she asked. "He knows we slept together. He could know about Lindsey."

"How would he know we slept together?"

"You told him." She could barely believe he was making her spell it out and came close to hating him. "To collect on your bet."

"Except I didn't." He appeared pained that she could believe anything of the sort; it was a performance worthy of an accomplished actor. "Like I told you, I didn't take any bet. I followed you from the party to make sure nobody else tried anything."

She had a mental flash of her and Ryan lying on the blanket he conveniently kept in the trunk of his car, gazing at the stars. She saw him turning to her, kissing her. She steeled herself against his feeble explanation. "You mean the way you did?"

"I only meant to take you home."

"Oh, please." She injected a wealth of sarcasm in her voice. Maybe *she* was the good actress because she managed to speak even though her chest was tight, the pain making it difficult to breathe. "Next you'll say you were only trying to get to know me better."

"That's the truth," he said. "Don't you remember how we connected that night?"

"You wanted to have sex with me," she accused, both her lips and her voice trembling.

"I was a sixteen-year-old boy. Of course I did." He placed a hand on her upper arm. "But if I'd planned it, don't you think I would have been smart enough to have a condom with me?"

Annie had wondered that exact thing and never come up with a satisfactory answer. As he said, though, he'd been sixteen years old.

"Teenage boys aren't known for thinking ahead." She shook off his hand and shouldered past him so he had to get out of her way.

"Isn't there anything I can say to make you believe me?" he asked, his voice laced with what sounded like desperation.

The birthmark seemed to sear the side of her cheek.

"No," she choked out and walked away from him into the house, refusing to look back.

CHAPTER ELEVEN

RYAN KNELT in front of the bookcase in his late father's basement study, pulling books off the shelves, opening them, then shoving them back into the slots.

"Try *The Teetotaler's Guide to Healthy Living*." Sierra stood at the entrance to the office, dressed in a short sleeveless nightgown, the walking cast on her left leg making her right one look thin and pale. He must really have been banging around not to have heard her approach.

"Excuse me?" Ryan said.

"Take my word for it and try it," she said.

He stood up, located the thick hardback book on the shelf, slipped it out of its niche and checked inside. The hidden compartment was there, the pages hollowed out. He reached inside and pulled out an empty flask. He held it up to Sierra. "How did you know this was here?"

"Probably the same way you did. I came down here once to ask Dad something and saw him taking a nip."

"How do you know he didn't tell me he had a flask hidden in one of his books?" Ryan said.

"Dad? I can't see it. He would have been too afraid Mom would find out to risk telling anybody." Their mother wouldn't hear of their father drinking a drop of alcohol after his first heart attack. "Besides, this family's good at keeping secrets."

"At drinking up the secrets, too," Ryan said ruefully. He put the empty flask back in the book and returned it to the shelf.

"Are you going to tell me why you're down here hunting for whiskey?"

"I didn't feel like drinking alone at the Blue Haven, and we don't have any alcohol upstairs," he said.

She crossed her arms over her midsection. "I've never seen you drink anything stronger than beer."

"Things change."

"Does this have anything to do with Annie?" At his questioning look, she said, "I know you're still seeing her. Chad told me he saw you together the other night."

He sighed. When had Sierra gotten so interested in his life? For years she'd been content to go her way and let him go his. She stood between him and escape from the office, clearly expecting an answer. "Yeah, well, I might not be seeing much more of her."

"Want to talk about what happened?" she asked.

"It happened a long time ago."

"I don't understand."

Of course she didn't. She'd been on the mark when she'd said their family was good at keeping secrets. They'd kept one from Sierra for fourteen years. Despite the small age gap and choice of the same profession, or maybe because of it, he and his sister had never been close. It had always seemed as if Sierra was competing with him. Most of the time he'd been content to let her win.

She seemed different tonight, standing there in her nightgown and walking cast. Softer. Easier to talk to. Maybe it was time to trust her with his secret, especially because a part of him longed to announce it to the world.

"There's a thirteen-year-old girl in town visiting Annie," he said. "Her name is Lindsey Thompson."

"She's the one taking care of that stray dog you picked up, right?"

"Right." Ryan took a deep breath. "She's my daughter."

The disclosure hung between them, filling the silence. He watched emotions flit across Sierra's face. The easiest one to identify was confusion.

"How could she be your daughter?" Sierra asked.

"I got Annie pregnant when we were both sixteen."

"No." Sierra turned pale. "You couldn't have. You weren't even seeing Annie."

"It was one time," he said. "It happened the night before I left for that year in Spain. You were at college when we found out she was pregnant."

"Nobody told me." She spoke softly, almost to herself.

"Mom didn't want anyone to know. Annie left town before the pregnancy showed, we gave up the baby for adoption and Mom never mentioned it again." He marveled that he could so easily sum up the events that had had such an impact on his life. "Hell, Annie and I didn't even talk about it until Lindsey showed up in town and Annie found out who she was."

He briefly filled in Sierra on the girl's surprise visit and Annie's agreement to date him.

"So what's between you and Annie isn't real?" Sierra asked. "It's all just because of Lindsey?"

"Not on my part, it isn't. Unfortunately I can't convince Annie of that." He'd told Sierra this much. He might as well confide the rest. "She thinks I slept with her on a bet some of the other guys made. I don't even know how she found out about it."

"Oh, no!" Sierra gasped and put her hands to the sides of her face. "She knows because I told her."

"What?" He couldn't process what his sister was saying. Sierra was many things but she'd never been cruel. "Why would you do something like that?"

"I heard some of the boys talking about it. I was just trying to warn her to be careful," she said. "I knew I was too late when her face turned white and she looked like she might pass out. I never imagined you were the one she'd slept with."

Ryan massaged the space between his eyebrows as things that had never made sense suddenly did. No wonder Annie had been so cool when he'd phoned her from Spain.

"I've felt terrible about it all these years," Sierra said. "Every time I ran into Annie, no matter how many years went by, I wanted to apologize."

"You couldn't have known," Ryan murmured, but he certainly wished he had. He would have called—or better yet, come home—and convinced Annie what had happened between them had been genuine.

Yeah, right.

He'd tried that tonight, and she hadn't come close to believing him.

"I'll talk to Annie for you," Sierra offered.

"It wouldn't do any good," Ryan said. "You can't prove I wasn't in on the bet."

"I'm so sorry," Sierra said. "Can you ever forgive me?"

Her face crumpled and tears welled in her eyes. Ryan crossed the room and put his arms around his sister, maybe for the first time in his life.

"There's nothing to forgive," he said. "It was high school. We were all kids. What did we know back then?"

"That's not the only thing I'm sorry about." She sniffled. "If I'd been in your corner back then, you would have told me about your daughter."

"You're in my corner now and I'm in yours," he said, holding her a little tighter.

They weren't the same people they'd been as teenagers. They'd both made mistakes, but they'd grown up. It was time to forgive each other the transgressions of the past.

That was it! Ryan thought with a burst of insight. That was what he hadn't seen clearly in all of this.

"I wish there was something I could do to help you with Annie," Sierra said.

"There is," Ryan said and proceeded to tell her exactly what it was.

LINDSEY RUSHED halfway up the sidewalk to the Whitmore house Thursday night, then pivoted and hurried a quarter of the way back. Quite a feat considering she was wearing her skinny jeans with wedge-soled sandals.

"Aren't you coming, Annie?" Lindsey called. "It's already past seven!"

Annie closed the door to the pickup, unable to muster the same enthusiasm as Lindsey. The confrontation she'd had the night before with Ryan was too raw, bringing up memories she thought she'd put behind her. She didn't relish seeing him again or telling him about the phone call she'd gotten earlier from Lindsey's stepmother concerning the girl's return trip home. She couldn't bear it if he persisted with the fantasy that they could have Lindsey with them always.

Annie was already feeling separation anxiety. She'd gotten too little time with the girl today, having spent the bulk of her day on the river guiding white-water trips after a morning appointment in town. A call from Ryan to Lindsey had dashed Annie's hopes to spend a quiet evening alone with Lindsey. He hadn't asked to set up a dinner date for himself but for his sister. It seemed Sierra had done some modeling in her teen years that Lindsey was dying to hear about.

"I'm coming, but I still don't understand why I had to drive you here," Annie said. The sidewalk leading up to the house was made of redbrick pavers, a classy touch on a property that transcended the ordinary. The landscaping was immaculate, the green blanket of grass neither too long nor too short. "It seems like it would have been easier on Sierra if I'd dropped you at the restaurant."

Lindsey giggled although Annie hadn't said anything funny. The girl had been doing a lot of spontaneous giggling since talking with Ryan earlier.

"Don't ask me," Lindsey said. "I didn't make the plans."

Annie didn't have a firm idea of what Ryan's plans for this evening were. She'd gotten the impression the dinner date was for two but she could be mistaken. Maybe Ryan would go along. He might even try to get Annie to accompany them. Annie would rather not be around either Ryan or his sister, but she'd gladly go to be in Lindsey's company.

"Annie! Come on!" Lindsey was already on the wide, spacious porch, ringing the doorbell.

The door, the fancy kind with the stained-glass insert, opened before Annie reached the porch.

Ryan greeted Lindsey with a big grin. Even from the bottom step of the porch, Annie spotted the love in his eyes. She could take issue with his treatment of her, but had no complaints about the way he dealt with Lindsey.

"I got Annie here," Lindsey announced, which was a strange way of putting it. How else would Lindsey have gotten to the Whitmore house?

"Hi, there, Annie." Ryan smiled at her as though last night hadn't happened. "Come on in."

She had the uneasy feeling that he was like a spider drawing her into a web, which was ridiculous. She couldn't have made it more clear that she wouldn't get involved with him.

The foyer of the Whitmore house was even grander than Annie had imagined, with gleaming wood floors and a curving staircase that ascended to a second-floor hallway. The dining room was off to the right.

Annie had envisioned the interior of the house enough times that she couldn't resist a peek. A crystal chandelier hung over a mahogany table. The light was set on low, the soft glow illuminating a table set for two. Tall, unlit candles added a touch of elegance.

"Surprise!" Lindsey cried, grabbing Annie's elbow. "While I'm having dinner with Ryan's sister, he'll be serving dinner to you! I almost told you about it a dozen times but I didn't."

"You did good, Lindsey." Ryan winked at her. "Thanks for getting her here."

Lindsey beamed. Annie simmered. Of all the underhanded tactics he could have used to get her alone, enlisting a child's help was the most grievous.

"Where's your sister, Ryan?" Lindsey asked excitedly. "I can't wait to meet her."

"She'll be hobbling along any minute now." Ryan didn't even have the humility to avoid Annie's glare. Her displeasure didn't even seem to affect him. "Ah, I hear her now."

Sierra's footsteps on the wood floor got progressively louder until she appeared. Annie sucked in a breath. Dressed in a short-sleeved top and a denim skirt, with her light-brown hair falling past her shoulders, Sierra looked even more like an older version of Lindscy than she had the last time Annie had seen the woman.

She stood silently by as Ryan made the introductions, afraid Lindsey would pick up on the resemblance. Lindsey was thinner than Sierra, her hair was a little lighter and her eyes blue instead of green, but the two females had similar bone structure and mouths almost identically shaped.

Emanating warmth, Sierra grasped Lindsey's hand. Sierra knew who Lindsey was, Annie realized with a start. Ryan must have told her.

Annie had difficulty getting through the next few minutes, although she managed to greet Sierra cordially and extend her wishes that she and Lindsey enjoy the dinner.

Sierra's boyfriend soon arrived to drive

Sierra and Lindsey to the restaurant, adding assurances that he'd pick them up when they were through eating. As soon as the three of them were out of the house and far enough away not to overhear, Annie spun on Ryan. "How could you?"

He shrugged. "I figured you and I had to eat, too. Why not together?"

"No." That transgression paled in comparison to his latest offense. "How could you have told Sierra about Lindsey? What if she lets something slip?"

Ryan didn't ask how she'd figured out Sierra was in on the secret. "She won't. She knows the deal."

"You saw them together. You must realize how much they look alike. What if somebody figures it out?"

"Nobody will figure it out," he said. "You saw the resemblance because you were looking for it. Now stop worrying and let's eat. I got takeout and it'll only stay warm for so long."

He left the foyer, heading in the direction of what must be the kitchen, as though she'd already agreed to have dinner with him. She glanced at the door, tempted to make her escape. If she did, how would she explain it to Lindsey? The girl surely expected her to be at the Whitmores' to drive her home after she and Sierra finished dinner.

"I could use some help," Ryan called.

She took one last longing look at the door, then trailed him into a spacious kitchen with granite countertops and stainless steel appliances. He must have swung by the dining room en route to the kitchen because he'd set the two plates from the table beside small white takeout boxes. Wordlessly Annie helped him transfer food from the containers to the plates.

"I went to that new Thai restaurant," he said. "I got red curry chicken and basil fried rice with beef. You can either pick one or we can share."

Sharing food with him seemed too intimate so she chose the curry chicken, keeping from him that it was her favorite Thai dish. He'd picked up some spring rolls and green tea, too, and seemed content to enjoy the meal. He didn't object when she turned the dimmer up on the chandelier, honored her request not to light the candles and didn't complain about her one-word answers when he attempted to start a conversation.

The meal over, she was helping him carry dishes into the kitchen when she couldn't stand the uncomfortable silences anymore. It would be best to get everything in the open. "What's going on, Ryan?"

He rinsed a dish, put it in the dishwasher and took the one she was holding before responding. "I don't know what you mean."

"Why are you acting like everything between us is fine?"

He continued to clean up, then said, "I'm acting like an adult."

"Could have fooled me," she said.

He ignored her sarcastic comment, drying his hands on a dish towel. "Last night I found out Sierra was the one who told you about the bet."

Annie felt her muscles seize up. "I don't want to talk about this again. There's nothing else to say."

"You might not have anything else to say, but I do. Sierra, by the way, feels terrible about what happened."

Annie had been about to walk out of the kitchen without hearing him out, but her feet felt frozen in place. "She shouldn't." Annie had never blamed Sierra for being the bearer of degrading news. "She didn't know we'd slept together."

"Exactly," Ryan said. "What struck me last

night was that her actions would have been forgivable even if she had known. Sierra's grown up now. We all are. Every one of us regrets some of the things we did when we were teenagers."

"You're saying we should be given carte blanche for everything we ever did wrong?"

"Not carte blanche and not for everything, but for the mistakes we own up to," he said. "Seeing you again made me realize what a jerk I was. I should have at least tracked you down to make sure you were okay after the baby was born, and I'm sorrier for that than you'll ever know. But I can't keep beating myself up over it."

He looked her straight in the eyes, the words seeming to come from his heart. She could hardly refuse to accept them. She nodded, waiting for the rest of his confession. Except he seemed to have finished.

"What about the bet?" She hadn't intended to mention it again, but the question slipped free. Tears immediately pricked the backs of her eyes. "Do you take responsibility for that?"

His head shook from side to side. "I've made enough mistakes. I'll be damned if I'll own up to one that wasn't mine."

His unflinching gaze met hers. She

searched his eyes for a sign that he was lying. Last night she'd claimed he couldn't say anything that would get her to believe him. It turned out his words hadn't done the trick. His eyes had.

He truly hadn't had an ulterior motive.

She thought back to that night, before Sierra had told her about the bet and the pain had kicked in. The connection between her and Ryan had seemed so real, the love-making special even though it had been her first time.

If he hadn't slept with her to win a wager, he'd done it purely because he was attracted to her.

The knowledge swept through her like a bright light, banishing the final remnants of the pain she'd held on to for far too long.

She knew enough about the man he'd become to believe he'd regret any past mistakes, but he wasn't guilty of the sin which she'd long attributed to him, and that made all the difference in the world.

"You believe me," he said softly. It wasn't a question.

She nodded anyway, hardly able to process her feelings.

"Yes," she said. "I believe you."

He closed the distance between them and framed her face with his hands. His gaze dipped to her mouth as though asking if he could kiss her. She raised her lips.

One of his hands slid from her cheek to cup the base of her skull. The other reached down so they were holding hands. His mouth lowered, claiming her lips with an unhurried gentleness.

It was the same as the kiss at the miniature golf course yet different. Time seemed to move in slow motion, magnifying every reaction. She could swear her heart had never beaten so hard, her legs had never felt so weak, her senses had never come so alive.

It wasn't because of the kiss, she acknowledged. It was because of the man.

Even when they were teenagers, before circumstance and misunderstanding had muddied the issue, the chemistry between them had been transcendent.

She opened her mouth, and he deepened the kiss, his tongue at first toying with hers until they were both no longer in the mood for playing. He slanted his mouth over hers, and she met his tongue thrust for thrust, her body molding against his.

Throughout it all, he held her hand, the

sweetness of the gesture touching her on a level his kisses couldn't.

She lost her bearings, where they were in the room being less important than their proximity to each other. She felt something against the backs of her thighs. It took a moment to realize it was the edge of the kitchen table.

"Ryan," she said against his mouth. "The table."

He blinked, seeming to realize where they were. He lifted her onto the table. She put her right hand down to brace herself and heard something crash. A glass vase. Flowers and water pooled on the floor.

"Oh, no," Annie said. "We need to pick that up."

"Leave it." He settled between her thighs and then he was kissing her again, the thrusts of his tongue and the heat of his mouth making her almost dizzy. He pressed against her, his erection unmistakable. The flat of his hand traveled from her waist to her breast. She moaned into his mouth and kissed him some more.

Finally he lifted his head. "We can't do this here."

Disappointment crashed into her. "I

know. Lindsey and Sierra could be back at any minute."

"They won't be back until at least ten." He sounded out of breath, barely in control. "I got Sierra to promise."

"You were that sure of yourself?"

"Not at all," he said, "but a man can hope."

She reached around his neck, intending to pull his mouth back down to hers, but met with resistance. She blinked up at him. "You're serious? We're really not going to do this?"

"We're not going to do it *here*," he said. "We're doing it in my bedroom."

He swept her into his arms like a modern-day Rhett Butler. She encircled his neck with her arms, holding on while he carried her up the curving stairs.

"If you drop me," she said, "it'll ruin the mood."

He laughed, holding her more securely against him.

"Why the bedroom?" she asked, her face buried in the softness of his neck. He smelled wonderful, like soap, warm skin and Ryan. "I would have done it in the kitchen."

"The last time I made love to you, I was sixteen years old," he said. "Like I said before, I'm not that same person anymore."

Yet he was. He laid her on his large mahogany bed when they reached his room, then they simultaneously embarked on a race to see who could get undressed faster. When he got his head stuck in his T-shirt, laughter slowed her down.

"I win!" he declared after finally struggling free of the T-shirt. She looked his nakedness up and down, appreciating his sculpted chest, his flat abs and his impressive erection.

"No," she said with a flirtatious smile, "I do."

He growled playfully, then came across the bed to help her remove the rest of her clothes. Then they were in each other's arms, reestablishing the connection they'd started to form on that long-ago night when Lindsey had been conceived.

Before Annie had found out about the bet, she'd considered that to be the best night of her life.

Not anymore.

This was.

WHEN RYAN got his sister to agree to stay away from the house until ten o'clock, he figured that would be plenty of time. With

Annie naked in his arms, he discovered it wasn't nearly enough.

Especially when she slipped away from him and started rummaging on the floor for her clothes.

He checked the wall clock, resenting the relentless ticking away of the seconds. "Come back to bed. We have twenty-five more minutes."

"Not if they show up early, we don't." She tossed a grin over her bare shoulder, looking so sexy with her tousled blond hair he nearly succumbed to temptation and pulled her back into bed.

"Not gonna happen." He propped his head on his elbow to watch her dress. "I told Sierra we had things to talk about."

He'd also informed his sister he aimed to get Annie to trust him.

Annie shimmied into a pair of hip-hugger panties. Next came her bra, which she put on with disappointing speed. At least there was a delicious intimacy in watching her dress.

"I appreciate that you have faith in your sister," Annie said, as she pulled on a sleeveless top that showed off arms toned from rowing, "but I'm not taking any chances."

Annie picked up her jeans. He sighed and

swung his legs off the bed, figuring he might as well get dressed himself. He'd rather their daughter not catch them in bed together.

Their daughter. He liked the ring of that.

"Do you know yet how much longer Lindsey is staying?" he asked.

"I've been meaning to talk to you about that," Annie said slowly. The mood in the room instantly changed from playful to serious. "She starts eighth grade a week from Monday. Her parents want her back with enough time to do some school shopping."

"How much time?" Ryan steeled himself to hear the answer.

"A week."

That meant Lindsey was leaving in four days.

"Her stepmother's checking the schedule," Annie continued. "She said she'd let me know which train to put Lindsey on."

He tugged on his pants, thinking about the situation at work. Sierra was supposed to get her cast removed tomorrow. If the nurse practitioner who worked part-time agreed to come in on Monday, together she and Sierra could handle the patient workload.

"If you line up guides to fill in for you on

Monday, Lindsey wouldn't have to take the train," he said. "We could drive her back."

Annie's hands froze at the waistband of her jeans, leaving them unbuttoned. Her body went equally still. "Is that why you slept with me? To get me to agree to talk to Lindsey's parents?"

Ryan jumped up from the bed and crossed the room to where she stood like a statue, stunned that she still didn't trust him. "I slept with you because I think you're amazing."

She stared at him, her eyes unblinking. "So you're dropping the idea that we should tell her parents who we are?"

"Well, no," he said truthfully. Was it so wrong for him to want the three of them to be a family?

"Are you sure one thing has nothing to do with the other?" she challenged.

The sounds of the front door banging open and footsteps on the hardwood floor carried from the downstairs. Ryan's eyes flew to the bedroom door. In their haste to reach the bed, they'd left it open.

"Ryan? Annie? We're back." It was Lindsey's voice, full of life and happiness.

Neither he nor Annie moved. More footsteps echoed, along with the thump of Sierra's walking cast, as though the two females were moving from room to room, searching for them.

"What happened in here?" Lindsey cried. "Look, Sierra, the vase is broken. Ryan? Annie? Where are you?"

"We'd better get downstairs." Annie moved away, putting distance between them that seemed symbolic.

He picked his T-shirt off the bed where they'd so recently made love and tugged it over his head, her question ringing in his ear.

Are you sure one thing has nothing to do with the other?

The hell of it was she'd created doubt where before there had been none.

CHAPTER TWELVE

RYAN REMOVED the patient's chart from the holder on the closed door Friday afternoon, glanced at the name and swallowed a sigh. Forcing a pleasant expression, he rapped three times and entered the examination room.

"Hello, Edie," he told the blonde who held a tissue to her nose. She was already positioned on the white-paper-covered table, her legs dangling in space.

Why was it that the person you ran into the most tended to be someone you least wanted to see? Edie Clark hadn't changed much from the girl she'd been in high school, the one who had made it her business to know everybody else's. It seemed that now she was omnipresent. At the pediatrician's office with her twin boys. At the miniature golf course with her family. And now here at Whitmore Family Practice.

"So what's the problem today?" Ryan asked.

"I feel terrible," she whined. "I caught the cold my kids had. They were sick for only a couple of days. It's going on four for me."

Great, he thought. *Yet another patient who thinks the medical profession has the cure for the common cold.*

He deliberately censored himself. If he hadn't lain awake last night unsuccessfully examining his motives for pursuing Annie, that uncharitable thought wouldn't have entered his tired mind. He'd gone into medicine to help people feel better, no matter how minor their complaints.

He got out his stethoscope and listened to her heart and lungs, checked her ears with his otoscope and asked her to open wide so he could examine her throat. Yep, she had a cold. He wasn't about to write out a prescription for antibiotics, but took out his pad anyway. He'd found that patients who visited the doctor for minor ailments liked to have a written plan.

"Rest and drink lots of fluids," he told her. "I'll jot down the name of a cough medicine I want you to pick up. You should feel better in a few days."

"Thank you, but it's tough to take it easy when you have three kids," she said, sniffling and coughing. "They're always wanting to do something. You should know. I saw you and Annie at the miniature golf course with that teenager who's visiting."

He made a noncommittal noise while he wrote. No way was he discussing Lindsey with Edie Clark.

"It was good to see Annie in town," Edie continued. "Writing for that magazine, she doesn't get back home much, does she?"

"Not much." He deliberately kept his response short.

"Until this summer I could count on one hand the times I've seen her since high school." Edie's throat sounded increasingly scratchy, but she kept talking. "I heard her father's retiring to Florida. Do you think Annie will move away for good after he sells the business?"

His head jerked up from the pad. "Excuse me?"

"Don't tell me you don't know the Sublinskis are selling their business! Annie was in town just yesterday talking to a real estate agent. Phil Mangini. He's married to my cousin."

"Are you sure it was yesterday?"

"Positive. I saw Annie coming out of Phil's office, plain as day."

Yet Annie hadn't said a word to Ryan last night about a potentially life-changing meeting with a real estate agent, not even after they'd slept together.

"I called my cousin and she told me Phil has a buyer lined up." Edie's voice gave out and she coughed, evidently to clear her throat so she could continue. "If the Sublinskis sell, and I don't see why they wouldn't, it'll be interesting to see if Annie takes that job in Australia."

Ryan had planned not to respond to Edie's gossip but couldn't stop himself. "Australia?"

She coughed some more, then nodded. "I hear the company that publishes her magazine also puts out something called *Outback Women*. I imagine after you work at the same place for so long, writing the same kinds of stories like Annie has, you're ready for a new challenge."

Could that be true? Was Annie really thinking about moving to Australia? It made a hazy sort of sense to Ryan and could even explain her reluctance to discuss the future.

"To each his own." Edie's voice was so hoarse he could hardly hear her, but she kept on talking. "But why anyone would willingly go to the Australian Outback is beyond me."

The thought of Annie leaving sliced through him like a hot knife. How could he possibly let her go when he'd just found her again?

She didn't even know yet that he loved her.

The realization slammed into him with a soul-deep certainty. Last night he hadn't been able to separate how he felt about Annie from his love for Lindsey. Now he could.

"You agree, don't you, Ryan?"

With difficulty he focused on Edie, amazed that she had been the impetus for his discovery, especially since he'd lost track of what she was saying.

"Agree about what?" he asked.

"The Outback. Haven't you seen those nature shows with the dingos and the heat and the bush? I mean, would you ever consider living there?" Her bloodshot, red-rimmed eyes widened. "You would, wouldn't you?"

Would he?

He stood up, ripped the top piece of paper off the pad and handed it to Edie. "Any grocery store or drugstore should carry that brand of cough medicine. Get some rest and you'll be better in no time."

He left the room without answering Edie's question. He was through talking to her, but once the office closed he had something very important to say to Annie.

He needed to tell her that he loved her.

ANNIE WADED toward the rocky riverbank in water that was calf-deep, pulling her kayak behind her. In the distance she could hear a police siren, a jarring reminder that life wasn't as tranquil as it seemed on the river.

The serenity Annie could usually count on when she was cloaked on all sides by water had been hard to come by today, though. She couldn't regret having made love to Ryan, but her feelings were as jumbled for him as his appeared to be for her.

It all came back to Lindsey.

She was terribly afraid she wouldn't be able to convince him they should keep quiet about being Lindsey's birth parents. Yet the girl's happiness could depend on it.

She dragged her kayak onto the bank, then motioned for the rafters in front of the pack to follow her lead.

The siren got progressively louder.

The flatbed trailer they used to transport the rafts to the put-in spot was waiting along with two high-school kids who worked part-time loading and unloading the boats. One of the boys was a head shorter and probably weighed forty pounds less than the other. He did the bulk of the work.

"Hey, Annie." Barry, the smaller, thinner boy, rushed up to meet her. "You better get up to the shop quick. There's trouble."

The siren's wail nearly drowned out his words. A police cruiser came into view, its tires kicking up dirt, sliding to a stop at an angle as though the driver was in too much of a hurry to straighten out the car. A longtime Indigo Springs cop she recognized as Joe Wojokowski got out and headed for the shop.

Had something happened to Lindsey? Annie's heart beat so hard she could hear the thump of blood in her ears.

"Lindsey," she breathed. The girl preferred staying at the shop with Hobo during the rafting trips. Considering that Jason had started treating Lindsey like a kid sister, Annie had been fine with the situation. "Is Lindsey all right?"

"Well, yeah." Barry seemed confused by her question. "She's not the one that customer has been yelling at."

The first rafters weren't yet off the river, but Annie would have to trust the boys to make sure they safely disembarked. She rushed up to the shop, the short distance seeming five times its normal length.

Lindsey met her at the door, Hobo at her heels. "I'm so glad you're here! I was just coming to check if you were back."

A very thin man wearing professor glasses and a straw hat that branded him as a tourist was gesturing angrily to the police officer, who everybody in town called Wojo. Behind the counter slouched Jason.

"This is unacceptable!" the man cried in a high-pitched, irritated voice. "I demand something be done about it."

"Excuse me." Annie approached the counter. She nodded to the cop, whom she'd known before his waist had spread and he'd started balding. She introduced herself to the irate customer. "I'm in charge while my father's out of town. What's going on?"

"I'll tell you what's going on," the man bellowed. "When I got back to the B-and-B, I discovered the camera equipment I'd left in my car trunk was gone."

"I just got here." Wojo's expression was almost bored as he chomped on a piece of gum. Peppermint from the smell of it. "He alleges the stuff was stolen while he was taking one of your trips."

"Alleges?" The man's face turned red. "I'm stating it as fact. My things were in the trunk when I left my keys with that smart mouth over there." He jerked his thumb at Jason. "Now they aren't."

"Smart mouth?" Jason's voice rose. "Was I just supposed to take it when you called me an idiot?"

"You *are* an idiot," the man retorted. "First you overcharged me, and now you're responsible for my camera being stolen!"

"That's enough," Wojo said roughly. "Name-calling won't get us anywhere. I need someone to tell me how this could have happened."

"Simple," the tourist said. "You take the keys, go into the parking lot and hit the remote. Whichever car beeps is your target."

"That shouldn't be possible. We have safeguards in place." Annie went on to describe their procedure. The keys were kept in a basket, then locked in a cabinet until the trip was over. Until now, they'd never had a single complaint.

Wojo turned to Jason. "You were in charge of the keys, right?"

Jason nodded slowly as though he didn't want to admit it.

"Then I'd say we have a suspect," Wojo said.

"Whoa. No way, man!" Jason exclaimed. "I wouldn't do something like that."

"From where I'm standing, it looks like you're the only one who could have done it," Wojo said. "Nobody else had access to the keys."

"That's not true!" Jason said. "Anybody could have taken them. I forgot to lock them up so they were there on the counter the whole time."

"You assured us that wouldn't happen!" the man exclaimed. "I never would have left my keys if I'd known you couldn't be trusted."

Annie cringed inside. Any moment now the rafters from the afternoon trip would start dribbling into the shop. She couldn't afford to have them hear about the unforgivable lapse.

"That doesn't leave you off the hook," Wojo said to Jason. "You still could have done it."

"I was in the shop the whole time," Jason claimed. "Ask Lindsey."

Lindsey had been standing unobtrusively at Annie's side, as quiet as a ghost.

"Tell 'em, Lindsey," Jason urged.

Lindsey wet her lips, hesitating slightly before answering. "Jason didn't leave, not even for lunch. He ate behind the counter."

Relief coursed through Annie that Jason

wasn't a thief, but they were no closer to solving the mystery of what had happened. The people embarking on the afternoon white-water trip arrived before the morning customers returned. Any one of them could have snatched the keys, stolen the camera, then returned the keys to the basket.

"What are the chances you can recover what was stolen?" Annie asked Wojo.

"Honestly?" Wojo shrugged. "Not good. Unless somebody saw who took the keys, I can't prove anything."

"That's unacceptable," the tourist fumed. "I won't stand by and let this happen. I demand—"

"I'll reimburse you the cost of the camera," Annie interrupted. "Just give me a way to contact you and I'll have my insurance agent call you. I'm sure he can take care of this to your satisfaction."

The bluster left the man. "Well, okay. I'll do that."

"I'll write up the report," Wojo said. "You'll need it for the insurance claim."

"Thank you," Annie said.

In the flurry of activity over the next hour, she barely had time to prepare for her inevitable confrontation with Jason.

Then, suddenly, she and Jason were alone in the shop. She might not be ready, but it was time.

Jason flipped his long hair out of his eyes. "I'm gonna take off if that's okay."

"Actually, I need to talk to you first."

"I don't have the money to pay for that camera, if that's what you're going to ask," he said.

"That's not it," Annie said, although she would have been in her rights. She took a deep breath. "Things aren't working out. I have to let you go."

He huffed out a breath. "You're freaking kidding me! Because I made one mistake?"

"You made a lot more than one mistake," Annie said. "You didn't get the bikes serviced. You usually come in late. Half the time you won't wear the company T-shirt. You're not exactly rude to the customers but you're not friendly, either. You don't even seem to like working here."

"That's a load of bull." Jason showed a fire he'd never displayed before. If he'd been this passionate about his job, things could have turned out differently.

"I'll mail your last paycheck," she said.

"You'd better," he growled, then he strode

through the shop, banging through the door and letting it slam shut behind him.

Annie sank onto the stool behind the counter and gazed down at the floor, massaging her forehead. She had too much on her plate. The demands of the business. Lindsey's imminent departure. And Ryan.

She still didn't know what she was going to do about Ryan.

She didn't immediately look up when she heard the door open, fairly certain Jason had returned to argue his case further.

"Annie?" It was Ryan's voice, filled with urgency. "Are you all right?"

He appeared before her as though he'd materialized out of the ether, but he looked strong and solid. And dear.

"I'm fine." She tried to summon a smile but found that she couldn't. "Okay, I'm not so great. It's been a really bad couple of hours."

"Does this have something to do with that kid who works for you? He looked pretty mad."

"He doesn't work for me anymore," Annie said, and told him what had happened.

He circled the counter and sat down on the stool next to her. "You did what had to be done."

"I know," she said on a sigh, "but it doesn't make it any easier."

"Running a business isn't easy."

"You're telling me. I'm thinking Dad should just go ahead and sell the place."

"So it's true?" Ryan asked, an edge to his voice. Although the cream-colored shirt and khakis he'd worn to work still looked fresh and crisp, he didn't seem like his usual cool, collected self. "You really do have an offer for the business?"

She was about to ask where he'd heard that, then figured it didn't matter. "I got a call yesterday from an agent who said he had a buyer if we were interested in selling. Since Dad's away, the Realtor asked me to come into town to talk to him about it."

"And?" he prodded.

"It's a good deal, especially with the economy the way it is and the business being seasonal," she said. "It takes a lot to run a place like this by yourself, and Dad's getting on in years. He might not be up to it anymore."

Ryan sat forward on his stool. "Why didn't you tell me about this last night?"

She shrugged. "I guess I didn't think it mattered."

"You thought I wouldn't care if your dad sold the business and you left Indigo Springs?" He sounded incredulous.

"I didn't think that far ahead," she said. "Besides, you might not stay in town. At the Blue Haven you said you had feelers out for a job."

"I'm keeping my options open," he said and paused before continuing, "in case I find myself contemplating a move to, say, Australia."

He gazed at her expectantly, his eyes never leaving hers, as though that should mean something.

"Australia?" she repeated. "Why would you move there?"

He frowned. "Doesn't the company you work for publish a magazine in Australia called *Outback Women*?"

"No," she said, shaking her head bemusedly, "but there is a mail-order catalogue called *Outback Women*. I've ordered clothes from them before."

She'd never seen another person's eyes grow so round. "Outback Women is a store?"

"I don't remember paying additional shipping charges, so I'm pretty sure it's based in the United States," Annie said. "Where did you get the idea it was a magazine?"

He threw back his head and laughed aloud, a noisy, boisterous sound. "From Edie Clark."

He sounded embarrassed. "She's the one who told me you and your dad were selling the business."

"At least there's a grain of truth to that." Annie felt as though she was missing something obvious. "What did you just say about moving to Australia?"

"I thought about it all afternoon," he said. "I even looked up how to become a licensed physician in Australia on the Internet. I was considering applying to the flying-doctor service that serves the Outback."

"You're not making sense."

He laughed again. "That's because I'm relieved that you're not moving to Australia to write for *Outback Women*. Because if you were, I was going to do my damnedest to find a way to come with you."

The air in the shop seemed to grow thicker, or maybe that was the lump forming in her throat. Last night she'd accused him of being interested in her because of Lindsey. Today he was offering to leave the country for her.

"Don't get me wrong," he said. "I'd rather stay in the United States, but I realized something when I thought you were leaving."

"What's that?" Annie could hardly get the question past her lips.

"You were wrong last night." He picked up her hand and gazed into her eyes. She could tell he was nervous. "Lindsey isn't the reason I want to be with you. I want to be with you because I love you."

A wave of happiness washed over her, but she fought it. She needed to think through this logically.

"It's only been a week since we saw each other again," Annie said. "Nobody falls in love that fast."

"We've known each other a lot longer than a week." Ryan's grasp on her hand tightened. He radiated sincerity. "I'm not saying I've been carrying a torch for you all this time. I haven't. I had feelings for you as a teenager, but that wasn't love. This is."

She bit her trembling lower lip, unable to believe him but unwilling to reject his claim that he loved her. She'd yearned to hear him say exactly that last night. She'd dreamed about it long before then, back when she was sixteen.

"I want to be with you, Annie, wherever you are." He didn't try to take her in his arms, perhaps sensing that she wasn't ready to make a commitment. "We can take it slow, if that's what you want. As long as we're living in the same city."

Another roadblock in a route littered with them. "I live on the road."

"What if you didn't?" he asked. "You love being on the river. What if you helped your father run the business?"

The suggestion was immediately appealing, especially since she wouldn't have to give up writing. She could dedicate herself to Indigo River Rafters in the warmer-weather months, work as a ski instructor in the winter and freelance whenever she found the time.

"I'm sure my sister would be agreeable to a partnership," Ryan said. "Think about it, Annie. We could both stay here in Indigo Springs. Together. It could work."

She stopped her imagination from taking flight and running with the idea, a danger when so many doubts still plagued her. "What about Lindsey?"

"We can figure that out later," he said. "You're what's important to me right now."

She let her hand remain in his, but her eyes must have conveyed her doubts. It was too much, too fast.

"I don't blame you for being slow to trust me." He drew in a deep breath. "Can you do something for me, though?"

She watched the emotions play across his

face. The only one she could positively identify was hope.

"Will you think about it?" he asked.

After a long moment, she nodded.

THE FLAT-SCREEN TELEVISION in the basement of the Whitmore house was a monster, fifty-two inches of high-definition digital picture that could highlight the most minute facial flaw.

The actors in the movie Annie was watching with Lindsey and Ryan Saturday night didn't seem to have any imperfections. Annie shuddered to think what the quality of the picture would do to her port-wine stain.

"Is it almost over?" Ryan sounded hopeful although it had been his idea to rent this particular movie and to watch it on the big screen his sports-junky father had bought before he died. Tonight no sports were on, unless Meryl Streep's ruthless treatment of her fashion-magazine staffers counted.

"Shh." Lindsey shoved a fistful of popcorn— low-fat, no butter—into her mouth. "I don't want to miss anything."

Ryan had missed quite a lot already. He'd nearly fallen asleep twice. Annie knew this because over the course of the movie he'd edged closer until his arm was around her and she was snuggled against his side.

Nobody had mentioned that Lindsey was leaving in a mere two days, but Annie felt sure it was the reason Ryan had gone to pains to make the evening special.

The fancy dinner at the nearby mountain resort had been a nice touch. Arranging to sit through a movie that didn't interest him for clothes-loving Lindsey's sake had transformed the evening into something out of the ordinary.

He was, Annie thought, the right kind of guy.

Last night he'd asked her to think about a future with him. Could she do that? She looked at him and saw all she'd ever wanted in a man. Could she pass up the chance to love him and be loved by him in return?

The closing credits rolled by on the screen, and Lindsey let out an audible, dreamy sigh. "Weren't those outfits great? I would love to wear stuff like that."

"You missed the point." Annie could barely focus while her mind was full of Ryan. "Meryl Streep's assistant was happier when she didn't look like a fashion model."

"Oh, I got that," Lindsey said airily. "Except I'd be happier *with* the wardrobe. I wouldn't want to write for a fashion magazine, though, although I think you should, Annie. I'd want the people at the magazine to write about *me*."

Ryan laughed at her cheeky statement. Annie was sitting so close to him, she could feel the reverberations travel down her own body.

"Nothing wrong with having aspirations," Ryan said. "Speaking of modeling, I thought I heard Sierra come home a little while ago."

Annie had heard her, too, even though Sierra had gotten the okay the day before to stop wearing her walking cast. A drawback to hardwood floors throughout the house was that they amplified noise.

"She said you asked her to look for the scrapbook our mom made of her ads," Ryan told Lindsey. "I was supposed to tell you she found it."

"Cool!" Lindsey shot to her feet. "I can't wait to see it."

She pounded up the basement steps, making enough noise to drown out the music that accompanied the movie credits. If she aspired to the runway, she'd have to learn to be lighter on her feet.

Ryan switched off the television, plunging the room into sudden silence. Now that they were alone, Annie expected him to raise last night's topic. She'd turned it over in her mind so many times her brain hurt. Should she speak up and tell him she'd decided to give their relationship a shot?

Is that what she'd decided?

He'd been idly playing with the hair at her nape, sending delicious shivers through her. Now his hand moved to her face, his fingers sliding lightly over her port-wine stain.

"You should have that removed," he said.

The delicious languor left her.

"There have been terrific advances in laser surgery in the past ten years," he said. "It may take a few treatments to get it completely taken off, but you could have it done as an outpatient."

If he'd slapped her, she couldn't have felt more stunned.

"I hadn't realized it still bothers you." Her throat felt so constricted she didn't sound like herself.

"Still?" He regarded her quizzically. "It's never bothered me."

"Then why bring it up?"

Offended when he didn't immediately answer, she jerked away from him, feeling as though she might double over in pain. After all that had happened, had it really come down to how he felt about her birthmark? "I should have known it would never work between us."

"Because I mentioned your birthmark? That's unfair!"

She got up and backed away from him, only stopping because she had no place to go with the big-screen TV behind her. "I should never have believed you loved me. If you did, you'd accept me just the way I am."

"I'm a doctor, Annie. I'm trained as a healer." He spoke slowly and deliberately. "I wouldn't have mentioned your port-wine stain if Lindsey hadn't told me you were self-conscious about it. I don't care whether you get rid of it or not."

She wrapped her arms around herself and rocked backward. "How could I ever believe that?"

He stared at her for what felt like a long time. "You know what I think? I think you don't want to believe it. I think you're using the birthmark as a smoke screen to keep me away."

Her blood pumped and her anger rose at his ridiculous suggestion. "Why would I do something like that?"

"Because you're afraid."

"Oh, please," she said sarcastically even though it felt as if her heart was breaking. "Protecting myself from getting hurt has nothing to do with fear. It's simply good sense."

"That's not what you're afraid of," he said. "You're afraid pursuing a relationship with me would mean telling Lindsey she's our daughter."

She started to say they couldn't tell Lindsey anything, then stopped herself, determined not to encourage his nonsensical argument.

"Hey guys," Lindsey called from the top of the stairs. "Come up here and see these photos of Sierra. They're really good."

They stared at each other in silence, his gaze challenging, hers defiant. Two nights ago he'd been her lover, but tonight it felt as though he was her enemy.

"You don't know what you're talking about," Annie said in as loud a whisper as she dared. "This isn't about me and Lindsey. It's about me and you."

"If that's all it was about, you'd be in my arms right now," he replied softly. "I know you love me. I could feel it the other night."

She refused to consider the possibility, casting about for another name for what she felt for him. "Attraction isn't the same thing as love."

"Okay, then," he said. "Maybe you don't

love me. Yet. But you're falling in love with me. And that scares the hell out of you."

"Of course it does," she all but hissed, heedless of what she was admitting. "You just told me I should have my birthmark removed. How was I supposed to react to that?"

"Like an adult," he said. "You could have said, 'Well, gee, Ryan, I don't think I will,' and the subject would have been closed."

"Annie! Ryan!" Lindsey called again, sounding impatient. "Hurry up!"

"I'll tell you what subject is closed," Annie said. "You and me. I'll get through the rest of the night for Lindsey's sake, but it's over between us."

She dashed up the stairs, angry at him for daring to psychoanalyze her. She was well rid of him. She ignored her traitorous heart, which seemed to break a little more with each step she climbed.

CHAPTER THIRTEEN

SUNDAY MORNING dawned bright, but Annie still hadn't banished the darkness of the previous night. She gazed into the bathroom mirror, her eyes instantly fastening on her port-wine stain.

Ryan Whitmore had a lot of nerve suggesting she was using the mark as a smoke screen. It was ludicrous to allege she'd rejected him because of some convoluted theory he had about Lindsey. Why couldn't he accept that her feelings for him weren't strong enough to overcome her mistrust and leave it at that?

She felt a tear trickle down her unmarked cheek and dashed it away. Lindsey was leaving tomorrow. Annie didn't intend to waste their final day together on tears.

She took a last look in the mirror, checking that her hair was in place and the makeup she'd used to cover the dark circles under her eyes was doing its job. She reentered her bedroom and put on a pair of strappy sandals that went well with her summery sleeveless dress. Lindsey had talked her into buying both on their shopping spree.

Annie had arranged to take the day off, although she hadn't thought past attending Sunday morning services. She was fairly sure Lindsey had phoned Ryan to invite him to meet them at church. She'd rather not see Ryan today, but it couldn't be helped. He had just as much right to spend this last day with Lindsey as she did.

Besides, she'd have to talk to him— again—about why it was imperative that Lindsey not know who they were. Refusing to consider the irony in that, she smoothed the skirt of her dress. If they didn't depart for church soon, they'd be late.

She left her bedroom, found the house quiet and rapped on Lindsey's bedroom door. "Lindsey! Time to go."

Silence answered her call. Annie listened, trying to determine if the shower in the en suite was running. The thickness of the wood prevented her from hearing anything. She knocked again, then cracked open the door.

A fresh floral scent, reminiscent of the bath

and body store they'd passed in the mall, filled the room. The door to the connecting bathroom was open, providing a view of a blue towel hanging crookedly from the horizontal bar outside the shower stall. Like the bedroom, the bathroom was empty.

Lindsey must have left the house while Annie was showering and getting dressed, probably to take out Hobo. Annie started to leave the room when she spotted one of her tennis shoes near the foot of the bed. Hobo must have dragged it into the room.

She entered the bedroom, bent down and picked up the shoe. While her eyes were level with the floor, she glimpsed another of her shoes from a different pair peeking out from under the bed.

"For pity's sake, Hobo," she said aloud.

She got down on her knees, retrieved the shoe and lifted the bedspread to check for any other missing items. Something glinted at her from under the bed. She squinted. Whatever it was seemed to be attached to a black object. She angled her body so she could see more clearly, but only succeeded in blocking the morning sunlight streaming into the room.

She extended her arm, her hand fastening on the object. It was square with something cylindrical extended outward. Something that felt like…a lens.

"Oh, no," she said aloud, and pulled an expensive-looking black digital camera from under the bed. The name of a famous company was printed in white letters above the telephoto lens. It was the same brand of camera that had been stolen from the angry tourist's trunk.

She heard a dog's joyful bark, then Hobo was skidding across the hardwood floor, going immediately for the tennis shoe Annie had dropped.

Lindsey trailed the dog, dressed for church in a sunny yellow dress. "What are you doing in my room?"

The girl's tone was accusatory but not worried, leading Annie to believe she must not have seen the stolen camera. She held it up in plain view. "What are you doing with this?"

Lindsey floundered, looking unsure of herself. "You shouldn't have been spying on me."

Explaining how she happened to be in the room seemed of secondary importance. "You shouldn't have stolen that man's camera."

"I didn't!" Lindsey said.

Stealing seemed out of character from everything Annie knew about Lindsey, but how could she possibly believe in the girl's innocence when she held the evidence in her hands?

Annie stood up. "You're making it worse by lying."

"I'm not lying!"

Annie ignored her. "I'll tell you what you're going to do. You're going to return the camera and apologize for stealing it."

Lindsey's face contorted. Her chest heaved in and out, then she pivoted and sprinted out of the room, through the house and out the screen door.

"Lindsey!" Annie shouted. "Come back here!"

The girl didn't listen, flying over the grass in her bare feet, Hobo barking and running after her. She must have removed her shoes after taking Hobo out.

The hour was too early for the morning group of rafters to arrive. The shop was open, though, a sometimes-guide Annie had talked into filling in for Jason having already brought out the rental bikes. Lindsey grabbed one and jumped on, looking incongruous with her bare legs and yellow dress.

"Lindsey!" Annie shouted again, but the girl was already heading toward the bike trail,

Hobo in pursuit, barking excitedly as if they were going on an excursion.

Annie stared helplessly after her, not sure where she'd gone wrong. She didn't even know whether to follow her or let her go.

She looked down at herself. She was wearing a dress and that silly pair of high heels. She couldn't very well chase after Lindsey outfitted like this.

She headed back to the house, berating herself all the way, her throat thick. She'd wanted to make memories today that could last her through the empty years to come.

She changed into shorts and a T-shirt, giving up on the notion of going to church. Her mind was whirling, trying to decide what she would say out on the trail if she caught up to Lindsey. Would it be smarter to wait until the girl came back on her own?

Smarter? Annie snorted to herself. When it came to how she dealt with Lindsey, the word *smart* didn't apply. She headed out of the bedroom, still unsure of what she was going to do. She sensed someone else was in the house before she saw the man standing in the great room, his eyes bleary as though he'd traveled all night, a suitcase at his side.

"Hello, Annie," he said.

She swallowed, futilely wishing she didn't have to deal with this now. "Hello, Dad."

LINDSEY PEDALED furiously, even though it hurt into her bare feet.

The trail was headed uphill, slowing her down so that Hobo caught up with her. The dog ran alongside the bike, his tongue hanging out like he was having fun.

Lindsey had been enjoying herself, too. She hadn't been looking forward to going back home. Home. That was the kicker. She'd felt more at home here than she ever had in Pittsburgh.

She still didn't think Indigo Springs was cool, but it had grown on her because of Annie and Ryan. *They* were cool. Or so she'd thought. She'd been wrong about Annie. She let out a strangled sob.

How could Annie believe she was a thief? She'd never stolen a thing in her life, not like some of her friends. They were always taking something when they went to the store, even if it was only a pack of gum.

She couldn't live with herself if she did something like that.

Sure, the camera under her bed looked bad. But Annie should have trusted her.

Annie hadn't let her explain that she was going to put the camera back in the man's trunk after spotting Jason stash it in the storeroom.

She liked Jason, even though he treated her like a kid sister. She didn't want him to get in trouble, so she'd taken the camera from its hiding spot. Before she could put it back, a customer had asked which sunglasses looked good on her. Helping the customer took so long, the man and his keys were gone.

Putting the camera under her bed had been a dumb move, but she hadn't known what else to do. Lying to the cop about Jason had been stupid, too. She'd almost confessed to Annie a half-dozen times yesterday. She'd meant to tell Ryan last night, but they'd been having such a good time she forgot all about the camera.

She pedaled some more, her legs hurting and her lungs burning. She wouldn't even be on the bike if Annie had let her explain.

Or, maybe, if she'd tried harder to tell Annie what had gone on.

Annie already listened to Lindsey more than her father or stepmother. If Lindsey went back, Annie would give her a chance to tell what really happened.

Hoping she was right, Lindsey stopped

pedaling and turned the bike around. She hurried down the hill, left the bike by the shop, then ran through the grass to the house where she'd been so happy. Hobo had gotten tired of following her and was chasing a butterfly. He'd be okay until she got herself out of hot water with Annie.

Her bare feet didn't make a sound on the porch. It hadn't been too hot last night so Annie had turned off the air conditioner, opened the windows and left only the screen door in place.

She heard Annie's voice and then an older, deeper male voice she recognized. She peered through the screen door. Annie was sitting on the sofa next to a thin man with gray hair. Yes! It was Uncle Frank. He was putting his arms around Annie. Was she crying?

Lindsey couldn't stand it if she was, especially if she was the reason. She put her hand on the doorknob, but she hesitated, trying to decide what to do. Her stepmother was always scolding her for eavesdropping but sometimes it was the only way Lindsey ever found out anything.

"Can you ever forgive me?" Uncle Frank asked Annie.

Lindsey's hand tightened on the knob. Forgive him for what?

"I gave birth to her, Dad," Annie said through her tears. "Don't you think I had a right to know you let friends adopt her?"

Who were they talking about? Who had Annie given birth to? Lindsey's heart thudded.

"I know, honey," Uncle Frank said. "But try to understand. I couldn't bear to give Lindsey to a stranger."

Lindsey couldn't breathe. Her heart seemed to stop beating.

They were talking about *her*.

It suddenly made sense why Uncle Frank had always paid so much attention to her. He wasn't her uncle at all; he was her grandfather.

And Annie was her mother.

Lindsey felt the blood rush through her veins. She gasped for air as the truth nearly choked her.

They'd lied to her.

Her dazed eyes fell on the purse and shoes she'd left on the porch when she took out Hobo. She picked them up and ran.

She thought about calling Ryan, but she quickly changed her mind. He was Annie's boyfriend. She must have shared the secret with him. Yet he hadn't told Lindsey, either.

She kept running, not sure where she was going or what she meant to do. Not sure of anything, now that she discovered Annie had betrayed her.

ANNIE SWIPED at her tears. She'd never been a crier and wasn't about to start now. Lindsey would be back soon and it was imperative she keep a clear head to better handle the problem of the stolen camera.

First she had to deal with her father. When she'd recovered from the shock of him cutting short his trip to Poland, she'd expected him to apologize for the past. Instead he seemed to have no concept of how wrong he'd been.

Annie moved out of his arms and scooted away so that the length of a sofa cushion separated them. She hardened herself against his hurt expression.

"You said the same thing on the phone about not being able to let a stranger adopt Lindsey," Annie said. "Except it wasn't your decision to make."

"Now, see, I don't agree with that." Her father's already lean face was drawn and pale, even though time in Poland with family he hadn't seen in years should have invigorated him. He was only sixty-five, but she could suddenly envision how he'd look as an old man. "I remember you asking me to make the decisions."

"Not about the closed adoption, I didn't." Annie's voice wobbled. "I was adamant about that. When I signed those papers, that's what I thought I was agreeing to."

"Why was a closed adoption so important? You never explained that."

Hadn't she? And yet she'd thought it was so obvious.

Annie didn't need a snapshot to see Lindsey in those moments after birth. The baby's dear little face had been red and she'd been crying, as though she somehow knew her mother was about to give her up.

Annie had been four years old when her mother gave her up for the first time.

"I know what it feels like to have a mother leave you." Annie's mother had treated their house as if it had a revolving door in the ensuing years, reappearing when she was low on money or luck. The visits had stopped abruptly when she got remarried to a wealthy Manhattan businessman. So had the birthday cards and the Christmas gifts. Annie had been nine. "I didn't want to put Lindsey through it again and again, the way it happened with me."

Her father sighed heavily as though the news didn't entirely surprise him.

"I wanted Lindsey's life to be idyllic, with two parents who loved her and never left her." Annie's heart squeezed at her naïveté. "It's ironic that it didn't turn out that way. When Helene died, she left Lindsey, too."

"Helene never would have left Lindsey by choice," her father said. "She loved her like crazy."

"Lindsey doesn't feel like she has that crazy kind of love anymore. Not since Helene died and her father remarried and had the boys," Annie said forlornly. "I wish more than anything she still did."

"She does have it," her father insisted. "I love her like that. And, more importantly, so do you."

Emotion clogged Annie's throat. He was right. She'd loved Lindsey with a fierce intensity since even before that wrenching day in the delivery room. Now that she'd gotten to know her, she loved her that much more.

"She's going back to Pittsburgh tomorrow," Annie told him, a wealth of sadness threatening to engulf her.

"Then go with her," he said. "Talk to her parents. Tell them who you are and say you want to be a part of her life."

His advice was exactly the same as Ryan's. Neither of them seemed to realize it wasn't that simple.

"Part of my reason for letting Helene adopt Lindsey was selfish, but not all of it," he continued. "When you were ready to be part of her life, I wanted you to know where she was."

Annie wasn't sure she could bring herself to believe him.

"I don't even know where she is right now," Annie said. "She was pretty upset when she took off on the bicycle."

"Then go find her," he said.

Knowing that was the best thing to do, Annie tried to find Lindsey, but she soon discovered the bike Lindsey had taken on her wild ride was back with the rest of the inventory. The girl was nowhere in sight. Neither was Hobo.

Jill, who was filling in at the shop, mentioned that a visibly upset Lindsey had asked to use the phone, saying her cell was dead. She'd called someone to pick her up, but the clerk didn't know who. Annie's best guess was Ryan.

Trying not to panic, Annie went back to the house and called him. His cell phone went straight to voice mail. The answering machine picked up at his home number.

Annie paced to the kitchen, where her father was pouring a cup of black coffee. "Ryan would have turned his cell off if they're in church. That's where we were headed this morning before I found that camera."

Her father arched one eyebrow. "Ryan knows about Lindsey?"

"It would have been wrong to keep it from him, Dad," she said. "Since Lindsey arrived, he's been spending a lot of time with us."

Something must have given away her feelings for Ryan because speculation entered his eyes. "Are you and Ryan together?"

"We were. We're not anymore." Her voice cracked, and she took a deep breath. "I'd tell you about it, but it's a long story and I need to check if they're in church."

"Tell me the short version then."

She inhaled, wondering how to sum up all that had gone wrong in a single heartbreaking sentence. "He asked when I was going to get my port-wine stain removed."

"Of course he did," her father said. "He's a doctor."

"But…" Annie began, then found she couldn't finish the sentence.

"To tell you the truth, I've often wondered the same thing myself," her father said. "I know it can be done."

Annie had no doubt her father loved her exactly the way she was yet she hadn't been willing to give Ryan that same benefit of doubt.

Because she was afraid.

Not only of being with Ryan, but of taking a chance that they could have Lindsey in their lives.

Just as he'd claimed.

Even now fear made her feet feel as if they were stuck in quicksand. She couldn't examine her motives for it or let it paralyze her, not when she wasn't absolutely sure Lindsey was safe.

"Will you stay here and call me on my cell if Lindsey shows up?" she asked.

"I'm not going anywhere," he said.

She ran out the door and to her car.

All the way she prayed for courage.

CHAPTER FOURTEEN

RYAN CHECKED the back of the church for what must have been the tenth time. In the row behind him, the elderly lady who'd taught him in elementary school had smiled at him the first two or three times. Now she made a circular motion with her index finger and pointed toward the pulpit.

The service was nearly half over. It seemed Lindsey and Annie weren't going to show, which didn't make sense. Why agree to meet him at church and then stand him up? No matter how Annie felt about him, she wouldn't have gone against the arrangements Lindsey had made.

Something wasn't right.

"Excuse me. Can I please get through?" He used a hushed voice to make the request of the couple standing between him and the aisle. He didn't wait for their answer, turning his body sideways and edging in front of them until he was free of the pew. He thought he stepped on the woman's purse, but heard her say something that sounded like "ow" and was pretty sure he'd gotten her foot instead.

"Sorry," he whispered.

Several members of the congregation regarded him with interest as he hurried down the aisle, driven by an urgency he didn't entirely understand.

Outside the church, Main Street was deserted, the shops and restaurants not yet open for business. The curbs along the primary thoroughfare and side streets were crammed with the cars of the people attending services.

Ryan switched on his cell phone, and an icon indicating he had a voice mail immediately popped up. Moving farther away from the church entrance, he started to press the button that accessed his messages when he saw Annie's familiar pickup pull up.

She got out of the driver's seat, leaving the door standing open behind her. His heart began to race. In tennis shoes, khaki shorts and a T-shirt, she clearly wasn't dressed for church. Lindsey wasn't with her, either.

He met her halfway, alarmed by the strain on her face. "Annie, what's wrong?"

"It's Lindsey," she said. "Please tell me she's with you."

His chest grew tight, and he now fully understood the blind panic associated with being a parent. "She's not. Why did you think she was?"

"She called somebody this morning to come pick her up."

The heaviness in his chest loosened but didn't abate. That didn't sound as bad as he'd feared.

"I haven't spoken to her since last night." He took her by the shoulders, feeling them tremble. He fought to keep a clear head. "Tell me what this is about."

He listened while she explained about finding the stolen camera under Lindsey's bed and their ensuing argument.

"I was going to give her a chance to explain when she got back from her bike ride except she took off again." Annie's face was pinched and drawn. "Jill—she's working in the shop today—said Lindsey was still really upset."

The story sounded off, and not just because it seemed wildly out of character for Lindsey to steal the camera. "If she had an explanation, why wouldn't she come back and tell you what it was?"

"I should have gone after her. I might have if my dad hadn't showed up." Annie stopped, her eyes growing huge and pained. "Oh, no!"

"What?"

"My dad cut his trip short so he could talk to me in person about Lindsey's adoption." She put both hands to her mouth. "What if Lindsey did come back? What if she overheard us?"

"Wouldn't you have noticed?"

"We had the screen door open. If she was standing on the porch, she could have heard everything." Annie looked as though someone had punched her in the gut. "Oh, Ryan. I mentioned you, too. What if she heard all of it? What if she knows we're her birth parents?"

Her theory would explain why he hadn't been the person Lindsey had called. He made himself focus. "Let's look at this logically. Lindsey knew whoever she called. We need to figure out who that was."

"Sierra?" Annie asked with audible hope.

"She's inside with Chad." He jerked his head at the church.

"How about Chase and Kelly?" Annie suggested. "Lindsey liked babysitting for them. You have a number for Chase, don't you?"

"I do." Ryan quickly got Chase on his

cell phone, but the forest ranger was at work on patrol duty. He gave Ryan his home number. The phone rang five times before Kelly answered.

Annie was white-faced when he hung up, anticipating his report.

"Kelly hasn't heard from her, either," he said.

"Lindsey must have overheard us," Annie said. "I was so stupid. I should have been more careful, especially after she eavesdropped that time when I was talking to Jason."

"Annie, stop." He took both of her hands in his. "You are not stupid. Far from it. I would not have fallen so hard for a stupid woman."

"Oh, Ryan—"

He put two fingers over her lips. "You don't have to say anything. Right now we need to find Lindsey."

She nodded once, and he took his fingers away from her lips. He tried to keep the heartache over things not working out with Annie at bay. Now was not the time to feel sorry for himself.

"Any ideas?" he asked.

"Just one," she said and told him what it was.

TWO HOURS later, Annie was out of ideas.

Considering she'd had only the single

brainstorm, that was not good news. She hadn't given up on her hunch that Lindsey was with Jason Garrity, but so far she couldn't prove it.

She'd had her father look up an address in Jason's employee file, but Jason wasn't home. Driving around Indigo Springs searching for his car, an older-model green Civic, also proved fruitless.

There was nothing left to do but return to the river rafters. She surveyed the familiar surroundings as they pulled into the dirt parking lot, trying to figure out what about the scene was wrong.

The trailers awaited the return of the morning rafting group, the mountain bikes were lined up outside the building and the river continued its timeless flow. The setting was awash in sunlight, a perfect enticement to tourists seeking to experience the sheer beauty of a day on the river, just like always.

A dog barked when they got out of the car, and she realized what was out of place.

Hobo was back.

"Hobo was with Lindsey, right?" Ryan asked just as the dog bounded toward him, putting his paws on Ryan's thighs, begging to be petted.

"Right," Annie answered as her eyes scanned the parking lot, zeroing in on Jason's green Civic.

The teenager suddenly was exiting the shop, swiping his long hair back from his face in a familiar gesture. That was when he saw them.

Ryan strode up to Jason, reaching him before Annie did. "Is Lindsey with you?" he demanded.

Jason scuffed one sneaker clad foot in the dirt, delaying his answer while Annie wanted to shake it out of him. "I took her to the train station in Paoli."

A vein in Ryan's temple bulged, but he kept himself under control. "You drove a thirteen-year-old girl to the train station and left her there?"

"Hey, she asked me to, okay? She said she couldn't stand it here any longer." Jason looked pointedly at Annie. "She said it was because you accused her of stealing that camera, but I'm not sure that was everything. She was pretty upset."

His observation was further confirmation that Lindsey had overheard Annie and her father. Annie's heart sank.

"Another reason for you not to leave her at the train station," Ryan retorted.

Some of Jason's bravado faded. "I didn't do so great. I realize that. But I asked the ticket-taker to keep an eye on her. Then I came here."

"To bring Hobo back." Annie wasn't willing to give him the benefit of the doubt.

"To tell you where to find her," Jason said defiantly. "Her train doesn't leave for another couple hours."

Annie nodded once, which was all the thanks she could muster. After shooting Jason a scathing look, Ryan grabbed her hand. "We should go."

She went with him toward the pickup, but they hadn't gotten more than a few steps when Jason called her name.

"There's something else I need to tell you." He looked down at the ground before lifting his chin and meeting her eyes. "I'm the one who took that camera."

She supposed she shouldn't have been surprised, but she was.

"I didn't even want the camera or anything, but that guy called me an idiot," he said. "I was just trying to cause him some grief."

"Why are you telling me this?" Annie asked.

"To get Lindsey off the hook," he said. "And because I needed to. I'll understand if you tell the police."

Annie was more likely to leave it up to the customer whether to press charges, but for now she was content to let Jason stew.

She and Ryan made their way to the truck. She handed him the keys, wordlessly asking him to drive.

"Let's go find our daughter," Annie said.

It wasn't just the first time she'd allowed herself to speak of Lindsey that way…it was the first time she'd thought it.

IT HAD only been ten days since Annie had last been at the train station in Paoli, but it seemed a lifetime ago. So much had happened, not only with Lindsey, but with the man driving her pickup.

Her feelings for Ryan were so jumbled she couldn't sort them out, but she did know one thing for certain—he had grown into a good man. A man she could count on in a crisis.

"Should I park first or drop you off?" he asked when the train station was in view.

He was really asking if Annie wanted to be the one to explain what Lindsey had overheard. That was only fair, she realized.

Annie had made the decision to give her up.

"Drop me off," she said, but hesitated

when he stopped the truck in front of the building. It felt as though her safety net had been yanked from under her.

He touched her cheek and met her eyes. "Go on. I'll be there in a minute. Everything's going to be fine."

She nodded, although once inside she was afraid Lindsey would never forgive her.

The train station was only a fraction as busy as it had been the last time she'd been there, enabling her to spot Lindsey almost immediately. She stopped dead, feeling her heart thump.

Her daughter was sitting in the same spot where Annie had first seen her. No, that wasn't true. The first time Annie had laid eyes on her she was a sweet-faced, crying newborn.

Lindsey was listening to her iPod, her eyes fixed on a spot in front of her. She wore the yellow dress she'd put on for church, but with her body slumped and her legs thrust out in front of her, she looked like a little girl instead of the young woman Annie had once mistaken her for.

She also looked miserable.

Drawing in a deep breath, Annie walked toward her. "Hello, Lindsey."

The girl straightened, her posture growing

rigid. She turned, and Annie could see the tracks of dried tears on her face. Lindsey shut off her iPod and took out her earbuds.

"Hello, *Mom.*" Her watery blue eyes muted her sarcasm.

Annie longed to take her in her arms and comfort her, but stayed where she was. The pain of being abandoned by her own mother had never really gone away. For Lindsey, the wound was fresh.

"I can explain," Annie said.

Lindsey didn't reply, continuing to gaze at Annie with that same downhearted expression. Annie wondered if she could say anything that would be sufficient.

"I never meant to deceive you," Annie said. "I didn't know you'd been adopted by friends of my father. I was just as shocked to find out the truth as you were."

"So it really is true?" Lindsey's voice shook and it seemed as though her whole body was trembling. "You really are my mother?"

"Yes," Annie said. "I am."

"Why didn't you tell me?"

"Lots of reasons," Annie said. "I didn't think it was my place. I wasn't sure how much your parents had told you about me. But mostly because I was afraid."

"Afraid of what?" Lindsey asked in a soft, hesitant voice.

"Afraid you wouldn't forgive me for giving you up." Annie moved to the bench and sat down next to her daughter, desperate to make her understand. "I was only sixteen years old when I got pregnant, seventeen when I gave birth. I couldn't give you the life you deserved so I asked my father to make sure you went to a loving family."

Lindsey said nothing, her huge blue eyes brimming with tears.

"Giving you up was the hardest thing I ever did," Annie said. "When the nurse took you away from me, it felt like my heart was being ripped out. That's when I understood what it was like to love somebody."

A few of the unshed tears in Lindsey's eyes escaped and trickled down her face.

"Oh, sweetie," Annie said. "Can you ever forgive me?"

Lindsey flung herself into Annie's arms, the tears flowing freely now. After a few moments, Lindsey said, "I was afraid you didn't love me. I thought you wouldn't care if I went back to Pittsburgh."

Annie held on to her for precious moments, then held Lindsey slightly away from her. She brushed back the hair from her daughter's face, awed that the girl had forgiven her so easily. "Of course I love you. We both do."

"Both?" Lindsey asked.

"Ryan's here with me," Annie said. "He's parking the truck. You should know that he wanted to tell you right off the bat that we were your birth parents."

"Ryan's my father?" Lindsey stared at her in obvious shock.

Too late Annie realized the girl must not have listened at the door long enough to hear that pertinent piece of information. She started to apologize, then thought better of it. Lindsey wanted the truth and now she had it.

"Ryan's your father," she stated.

Out of the corner of her eye, Annie caught Ryan striding toward them. "There he is now."

Lindsey's head whipped around, then she looked back at Annie in awe.

"Ryan's my father," Lindsey repeated, the words no longer a question but a statement.

She scrambled to her feet and practically flew across the floor of the train station, flinging herself into Ryan's arms. He hugged her and twirled her around, father and daughter wearing identical expressions of joy.

A lump of emotion formed in Annie's throat

while she watched the joyous scene between two of the people she loved most in the world.

THE DRIVE back to Indigo Springs passed in a blur for Annie, with Lindsey asking countless questions about their family trees.

Lindsey already knew that Annie was an only child and Ryan had one unmarried sister, but she was eager to hear about grandparents and cousins.

Other than agreeing that Ryan and Annie would drive her back to Pittsburgh, none of them mentioned the future.

It stretched ahead of them like the great unknown, making Annie's anxiety grow with each passing mile. Back at the train station she'd realized she loved Ryan, but she very much feared she'd killed whatever love he might have had for her.

Lindsey took hold of both of their hands when they reached the river raft compound, skipping between them like a young child. She didn't let go until they were inside the house and Annie's father got up from the sofa where he'd been waiting for them.

"Hi, Grandpa," Lindsey called, running ahead of them to catapult herself into his arms while Hobo danced around them.

Her father had made this possible, Annie thought as she watched him clutch his only granddaughter to him. If she hadn't forgiven him before, she did now.

"How about you and me take your mutt for a walk?" her father remarked to Lindsey after greeting Ryan. He winked at Annie. She didn't know how, but he must have realized how much she and Ryan had to discuss.

And then, suddenly, Annie and Ryan were alone.

"Why don't we wait for them on the porch?" Annie suggested. They sat in side-by-side rockers that overlooked the rippling river, protected from the still-bright sun by the overhang.

Lindsey called it a granny porch. Annie wouldn't mind growing old, she thought, if Ryan was by her side.

"We need to talk about how to handle tomorrow," Ryan said when her father, Lindsey and Hobo disappeared on the trail at the far end of the property.

His comment jarred Annie back to reality. He was right. She needed to focus on tomorrow and their daughter, not some flight of the imagination of a future with Ryan. She'd already ruined that.

"Only Helene knew that my father was more than just a family friend," she said. "It'll be a shock for Lindsey's father and step-mother to find out we're her birth parents. There's no getting around that."

"That's true," Ryan said. "But Lindsey isn't a baby. She'll have a lot of say in what happens next."

"She'll want us to be part of her life," Annie said. "That was obvious from how she reacted this morning."

"We'll make sure her father and step-mother know our split was amicable," he said. "We'll convince them we don't want to interfere. We just want to see Lindsey from time to time. Have her visit Indigo Springs."

Split... Amicable. He'd used two of the words most commonly associated with divorce. Pain stabbed at Annie, seeming to center in her heart. Just days ago she'd tumbled back into love with him, and now they were at this sad place.

What's more, it was her fault.

"I'm sorry," she blurted out.

He cocked his head. "Sorry for what?"

"Those things I said when you asked about my port-wine stain. You were right. I was afraid being with you would mean being a mother to Lindsey, and I didn't think I could do that."

"Why not?" he asked, his eyes intent on hers.

"I thought I might be as bad at it as my mother was. After all, I gave Lindsey up, just like she gave me up." Annie took a deep breath. Now that Lindsey had forgiven her sin, she found she could forgive herself. She could even understand it. "When Lindsey went missing, I realized I was nothing like her. My mother never cared enough to be part of my life. I knew that if we were lucky enough to find Lindsey, I'd do anything to stay in her life. It's what I want more than almost anything."

"*Almost* anything?" he asked, fastening on the qualifier. "What is it you want more than that?"

She wet her lips, wondering if she'd have the courage to tell him. "For you to forgive me for the ugly things I said."

"Done." He got up from his rocking chair, stood in front of hers and pulled her to her feet. While holding her hands, he looked into her eyes. "I could forgive you anything, Annie. I love you."

"You still love me?" She could barely make herself believe it, but his familiar blue eyes were smiling, like his lips.

"I started to fall in love with you fourteen years ago," he said. "Did you really think I'd get over it in a couple of days?"

"Well, yes," she admitted.

He placed one of her hands over his heart, which was racing just like hers.

"Feel what you do to my heart, Annie," he said, "because you're in there to stay."

Her gasp was both a cry of relief and joy. She lifted her lips, expecting his mouth to cover them. His kiss, soft and warm, landed on her port wine stain instead.

"One more thing," he said when he lifted his head. "I love you, Annie Sublinski, just the way you are."

He smiled. This time, when he kissed her, it was on the lips.

EPILOGUE

Six months later

POWDERY white snow stretched as far as the eye could see, coating the evergreens and sloping trails where skiers zigzagged down the mountainside.

Sitting in a ski lift with Ryan on one side of her and Lindsey on the other, Annie watched her warm breath turn visible in the cold winter air when she laughed.

"You'll have to let go of my arm to get off the ski lift, Lindsey," Annie told her daughter.

"I don't think I can," Lindsey muttered. "I don't know why I let you talk me into leaving the beginner hill."

"Because Annie's working here as a crackerjack ski instructor and she says you're ready." Ryan leaned slightly forward and directed his comment at Lindsey, then grinned at Annie.

Staying in Indigo Springs to help her father run the river rafters was only one of the decisions Annie had made since last summer. Because the business was seasonal, she'd had to find a job to keep her occupied during the winter months.

The ski resort where her father worked as director of ski operations in the river rafters' off season fitted the bill perfectly. Her schedule was flexible enough to write the occasional freelance story for *Outdoor Women* and to spend plenty of time with Ryan, who was now a full partner at Whitmore Family Practice.

The only drawback was the gobs of ointment she needed to slather on her cheek where her port-wine stain had been to protect the skin from the winter sun.

"I'm not ready." Lindsey held herself perfectly still, her legs in her pink ski pants and new boots the only parts of her body that moved as they swayed slightly in the winter breeze. "I should have stayed home with Sierra."

By *home,* she meant the grandiose Whitmore house in downtown Indigo Springs. The house where Annie still lived with her father had only two bedrooms so they'd decided it made more sense for Lindsey to stay with Ryan on her frequent visits.

"You'll be fine," Annie said.

"Do we have to get off at the top of the mountain?" Lindsey asked as the disembarkation spot got closer. "Can't we just stay on the lift and go back to the bottom?"

"It doesn't work that way," Annie said. "We have to get off."

That fact didn't seem to get through to Lindsey. "But if I break my leg, my other dad might not let me move to Indigo Springs this summer."

It turned out that Lindsey's adoptive father really did love her, enough that he'd surrendered to her pleas to live primarily with Annie and Ryan. She'd start high school at Indigo Springs High, but the Thompsons weren't giving her up entirely. The plan was for Lindsey to spend one weekend a month, alternating holidays and two weeks of every summer in Pittsburgh.

"Then we'll make sure you don't break a leg," Ryan said.

"It'd be a shame if our maid of honor needed crutches to walk down the aisle," Annie said, then turned to Ryan. "Can you believe our wedding is only two days away?"

"If it were up to me, we'd already be married," he said.

"It takes time to plan a big wedding." Lindsey put her anxiety on the back burner to give him an eye roll. "How many times do I have to tell you that, Ryan?"

Annie laughed. "Listen to her, Ryan. She's the one who got us back together after all."

"And don't you forget it," Lindsey said.

Annie looked around their daughter to smile at Ryan. She would have leaned over and kissed him if it hadn't been almost time to get off the ski lift.

"Oh, no!" Lindsey cried. "I can't remember what to do!"

"Point your poles forward and lift the tips of your skis," Annie said as the horizontal bar automatically lifted. "Stand up after the chair passes over the top of the mound. And let go of my arm."

Lindsey complied but not without a girlish squeal. She did as Annie had instructed, managing to stay upright as all three of them successfully got off the lift.

"That wasn't so bad now, was it?" Annie asked. "Keep listening to me and we'll make a skier out of you yet."

Lindsey sniffed. The cold had turned her

cheeks pink to match the insets in her sleek black ski jacket.

"If I do this," she said, gazing down the mountain, "both of you have to come with me when your wedding photographer takes my modeling pictures."

"Fine with me," Annie said.

"Me, too," Ryan said, exchanging a conspiratorial wink with Annie.

Lindsey trudged ahead of them, walking awkwardly on her skis.

"So I'm just supposed to let the gravity take me, right?" Lindsey asked. "Why don't you go before me… Whoa! I can't stop!"

She stayed upright, positioning herself at an angle as Annie had taught her, moving over snow turned even whiter by the glare of the sun.

Annie slanted a proud grin at the man she loved, then the two of them followed their daughter down the mountain and into the bright future.

* * * * *

RICK'S APPOINTMENT with his attorney early Wednesday morning went only moderately better than his meeting with social services the day before. The prognosis wasn't great—but at least his attorney was going to file a motion for DNA testing. Just so Rick could petition to see the child…his sister's baby. The sister he didn't know he had until it was too late.

The rest of what his attorney said had been downhill from there.

Cell phone in hand before he'd even reached his Nitro, Rick punched in the speed dial number he'd programmed the day before.

Maybe foster parent Sue Bookman hadn't received his message. Or had lost his number. Maybe she didn't want to talk to him. At this point he didn't much care what she wanted.

"Hello?" She answered before the first ring was complete. And sounded breathless.

Young and breathless.

"Ms. Bookman?"

"Yes. This is Rick Kraynick, right?"

"Yes, ma'am."

"I recognized your number on caller ID," she said, her voice uneven, as though she was still engaged in whatever physical activity had her so breathless to begin with. "I'm sorry I didn't get back to you. I've been a little…distracted."

The words came in more disjointed spurts. Was she jogging?

"No problem," he said, when, in fact, he'd spent the better part of the night before watching his phone. And fretting. "Did I get you at a bad time?"

"No worse than usual," she said, adding, "Better than some. So, how can I help?"

God, if only this could be so easy. He'd ask. She'd help. And life could go well. At least for one little person in his family.

It would be a first.

"Mr. Kraynick?"

"Yes. Sorry. I was…are you sure there isn't a better time to call?"

"I'm bouncing a baby, Mr. Kraynick. It's what I do."

"Is it Carrie?" he asked quickly, his pulse racing.

"How do you know Carrie?" She sounded defensive, which wouldn't do him any good.

"I'm her uncle," he explained, "her mother's—Christy's—older brother, and I know you have her."

"I can neither confirm nor deny your allegations, Mr. Kraynick. Please call social services." She rattled off the number.

"Wait!" he said, unable to hide his urgency. "Please," he said more calmly. "Just hear me out."

"How did you find me?"

"A friend of Christy's."

"I'm sorry I can't help you, Mr. Kraynick," she said softly. "This conversation is over."

"I grew up in foster care," he said, as though that gave him some special privilege. Some insider's edge.

"Then you know you shouldn't be calling me at all."

"Yes… But Carrie is my niece," he said. "I need to see her. To know that she's okay."

"You'll have to go through social services to arrange that."

"I'm sure you know it's not as easy as it sounds. I'm a single man with no real ties and I've no intention of petitioning for custody. They aren't real eager to give me the time of day. I never even knew Carrie's mother. For all intents and purposes, our mother didn't raise either one of us. All I have going for me is half a set of genes. My lawyer's on it, but it could be weeks—months—before this is sorted out. Carrie could be adopted by then. Which would be fine, great for her, but then I'd have lost my chance. I don't want to take her. I won't hurt her. I just have to see her."

"I'm sorry, Mr. Kraynick, but..."

* * * * *

Find out if Rick Kraynick will ever have a chance to meet his niece.
Look for A DAUGHTER'S TRUST by Tara Taylor Quinn, available in September 2009.

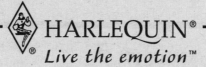

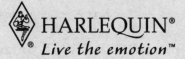

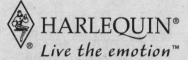

HARLEQUIN®
INTRIGUE®

BREATHTAKING ROMANTIC SUSPENSE

Shared dangers and passions lead to electrifying romance and heart-stopping suspense!

Every month, you'll meet six new heroes who are guaranteed to make your spine tingle and your pulse pound. With them you'll enter into the exciting world of Harlequin Intrigue— where your life is on the line and so is your heart!

THAT'S INTRIGUE— ROMANTIC SUSPENSE AT ITS BEST!

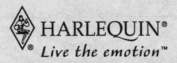

HARLEQUIN®
Live the emotion™

www.eHarlequin.com

INTDIR06

![Harlequin Historical logo] **Harlequin® Historical**
Historical Romantic Adventure!

*Imagine a time of chivalrous
knights and unconventional ladies,
roguish rakes and impetuous
heiresses, rugged cowboys
and spirited frontierswomen—
these rich and vivid tales will
capture your imagination!*

*Harlequin Historical...
they're too good to miss!*

♥ Silhouette®

SPECIAL EDITION™

Emotional, compelling stories that capture the intensity of living, loving and creating a family in today's world.

Special Edition features bestselling authors such as Susan Mallery, Sherryl Woods, Christine Rimmer, Joan Elliott Pickart— and many more!

For a romantic, complex and emotional read, choose Silhouette Special Edition.

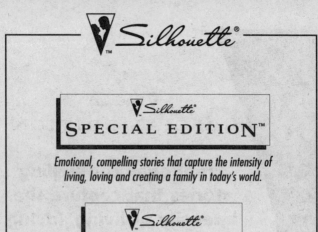

SPECIAL EDITION™

Emotional, compelling stories that capture the intensity of living, loving and creating a family in today's world.

Desire

Modern, passionate reads that are powerful and provocative.

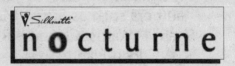

nocturne

Dramatic and sensual tales of paranormal romance.

Romantic SUSPENSE

Romances that are sparked by danger and fueled by passion.

SDIR07